About the Author

Creatively, Ferdinand Jensen has been working on writing, mosaic, music, and painting. He is fairly young and lives in South Africa and speaks German and English. He is fascinated by how the mind works and cannot get enough of compositions and lively depictions of figments in reality.

Shades & Hues

Ferdinand Jensen

Shades & Hues

Olympia Publishers
London

www.olympiapublishers.com
OLYMPIA PAPERBACK EDITION

Copyright © Ferdinand Jensen 2024

The right of Ferdinand Jensen to be identified as author of
this work has been asserted in accordance with sections 77 and 78 of
the Copyright, Designs and Patents Act 1988.

All Rights Reserved

No reproduction, copy or transmission of this publication
may be made without written permission.
No paragraph of this publication may be reproduced,
copied or transmitted save with the written permission of the publisher,
or in accordance with the provisions
of the Copyright Act 1956 (as amended).

Any person who commits any unauthorised act in relation to
this publication may be liable to criminal
prosecution and civil claims for damage.

A CIP catalogue record for this title is
available from the British Library.

ISBN: 978-1-80074-866-8

This is a work of fiction.
Names, characters, places and incidents originate from the writer's
imagination. Any resemblance to actual persons, living or dead, is
purely coincidental.

First Published in 2024

Olympia Publishers
Tallis House
2 Tallis Street
London
EC4Y 0AB

Printed in Great Britain

Black Space

This expanse that apparently contains just nothing but stars and planets. Dying when exposed to it – it has a dangerous undertone of mystery, unknowing and essences of the beyond.

We stare at it for long times until we get it anew every time. It is the answer you get from seeking. For no reason asking yet again. Endless in its nature, it's speckled with life of miraculous nature in so many forms – I think it's there to broaden imagination.

The infatuation with black holes within it promises even more – do they lead somewhere, or do you just meld into formless existence when you go inside?

The concept of even more nothingness being out there – just more and more of it. It has to consist of something – do we feel it while meditating or does it feel like death? Is that what we become once we reach the end?

Glad that it is filled with substance it coldly holds life in its embrace – a formless, never-ending frame.

Without the concept of nothing, how can there be something? An age-old question that begs the answer: there is no such thing as nothing. It's a conundrum that bugs the mind, and ironically there is so much of it.

Emptiness, yet so full – we will never stop wondering and exploring.

In its nature is the energy of always finding more.

Just imagine what horrors and miracles we can find within

it – I close my eyes and each time stars let me know there is no giving up hope. Do I find pleasure in the unknown? Is it really the same darkness I experience each time?

It's different when I close my eyes again – each millisecond of change makes the entire canvas that tiny bit better. Life just gets better and better as you live it, is this what space knows? As I expand and go along in my black way, I make things better.

Unfathomable it will stay, a source of endless imagination-food.

Black v1.0

Painfully I have lived this life and sadly it is not over yet... I am merely in the middle of it – screaming from my heart-centre through the charred skin I call this shell of a spirit I am.

A crusader in hell, only being fed when there are scraps left and continuously quenching my never-ending thirst when the flames have gotten too deep.

Through this constant battle I fight, with no end in sight. It is the path that is so pleasant to me – every day I awaken to yet another brawl and every evening I emerge victorious.

When the outside influence stops, my conscience takes over and the stakes are raised.

How well can I fend off the attackers before there is time to recuperate again? A hardened exoskeleton I have built, and my tracks are stomped into the dust behind me – all the way to my first steps.

It is I, that memorizes this existence – the only one that cares for my own wellbeing in a way that is cold-hearted enough to allow growth, wild-hearted enough to procure adventure and simmering to yield rest.

Pointless thoughts of endings and better times plague me here and there, but I treat them as givens – innately you become better at what you do. It is the worth of the experience and the quality of life you live in, that matters. By now I feel like an immense rock that is being steered by forces unknown.

A blunt arrow, designed to stun or cripple when breaking

its victim is what I seek to be. Shot out with the crossbow of vindication and meeting its mark in the heart of deciphered and refined certainty.

How do we analyse correctly and when do we kill the mockingbirds that are doubt, spiritual weakness, idiocy, unknowing and mystery? The stupid childish mind that always proposes something new and unexplored is undermining professionalism in the tiny areas we, at least, have some knowledge of.

I am making progress in this life, no matter what the cost – I feel it in my nervous system, just unyieldingly resonating this energy that has me expend anew. Like an everblooming flower in a time-lapse that has it open again and again.

Closing the circle, I put this flow into the foundation of my being and call it a part of my indomitable spirit.

Dangerous Blackness

The intent is what scares the most, it's palpable in the spirit. This feeling of evil being inflicted unto the core, unkind and unforgiving.

The absence of empathy along with violent and harmful stabbing at the soul must be the worst way to die. To make matters worse the imagination is as bad as it happening for real – in fact if it were for real there would be release thereafter.

We imagine worse than what life actually is, yet life is often worse than we imagine. Why are the two so intrinsically linked? How I wish I could dislocate my mind from my head and just go with my heart and peace where my thoughts were.

Thinking feels like a disability right now – at the cusp of another minor freak out session that manifests some of the most evil darkness there is. Uncontrollable and belligerent the mind pounds bullet for bullet into skull, remorseless and unknowing of anything better.

It's these spirals that eventually have effect on the physical existence. I am fearful of overthinking, so I clench – suffocating the root.

As if going through a brochure I wish on my end being creative as if it were in my control. Can I really decide how I die and how much does it actually mean? Does obsessing about it help anything? What's true is that fear of death has long ago stopped being the prime motivator for thinking about it – it's more of a nuisance than anything.

The world keeps mentioning endings simply out of cruelty, to point of boredom. Keeping the danger ever at bay seems to be a skill you learn while growing up – once you're adult, you know how. Once you've gotten to know it, there is this protective force that sways your choices at nearly every turn.

What you have come for is release from fear through realization – do you wish to realize your fear or realize the fear is useless? In its nature most fear is irrational and since it's self-created; it can be controlled.

Mitigation until the end – this invokes imagination of a downward spiral, yet philosophy will have you rethink that into a continuous motion of realizing every spiral each thought creates as the sediment, forms part of your base.

So, eventually you will have to work on multiple levels to not have some kind of dire ending. Why does death always bring sadness mostly? Is it peer pressure or just cultivated behaviour?

All too used to something bitter – there's even a taste for it.

Black v2.0

Classy I feel like, streamlined and shiny. A sort of elegance I have now. As I exonerate myself from the crowd in my awareness, I become untouchable.

Bear witness to my ability – I have risen beyond. This statement I flaunt in unmistakeable style so that you may know beyond any doubt that there is someone worthy of noting in your presence.

Being the one that shows and creates the contrast in the world, so you may see the difference, is where my intent lies. Without me you are nothing, and I hope you factor that into your conscience before you address me.

Above the silliness you exude I am inflicting unto you the knowledge of being in the presence of someone that has superseded you. My wish is for the ones that dare gaze upon me to feel the feelings of inadequacy and suffer at their inferiority complexes.

You will start doubting when you see me. Right to the point where you question reality.

Omega is my unspoken name and I insist on hush tones whispered through the underground. You may create the hype, the paranoia, the speculation…

See if your notions compare.

There is nothing you can prove and attempting to cage me is futile, for I am bolstered. Fearlessly I invoke fear in others and those who do not respect me yet suffocate at their own wills to thwart me.

Before I vanish, you may see a glint from my exterior, to let you know that the opposite does, in fact, exist.

Black With Attitude

I'm over my dark side and I wear it with pride. Above the drama that is life and death, I know my place in the cycle. There is a certain energy to completion, and I'll start feeling it once the time is right, so for now I'll stride – just oozing myself into the world.

Dressing as the shade of myself, it's how I have come to know the world in its rugged and gritty state. No remorse for right-doing, people can see where the chips fall once I have had my way. Bulldozing and cutting my jagged path, there is clarity within my intent.

The weak might say I do not care, but it's a matter of principles – like a drug deal you pay the price; or you get scarred. I make my own rules – taught by the world, there is no such thing as letting myself be taken for a ride.

The anvil is the colour of my clothes because it represents an unbreakable force. Deep into my bones I have been chiselled into this unforgiving state. There is a lack of open kind-heartedness about me, yet the status of giving has yielded a culture abusing this trait mockingly.

The unsung hero with brutal morals is undeniably correct in his own perspective, while the politics around his actions don't touch him. Burning his way through the dead, sharp grassland he leaves nothing but ash behind.

You will come to fear my arrival in your life – for it brings reckoning.

My departure will hallow your knowing of where you stand as if branded.

Black v3.0

Underneath it all there is stillness, an empty canvas in which we choose to shine light onto – agitating it to become something vibrant or whatever...

I prefer the darkness to be the backdrop – it's just more natural. We spring from unliving into living and so every start has to be. Are we turning things on their head when starting with white? In my perception there has been too much that has been birthed from darkness to accept that we start in what shines. Don't WE shine the light?

When there is nothing, it creates the opportunity to become, and so the something must be. Maybe it's a mere point of view that appreciates what has not been yet, that gives rise to so much love for life.

To holistically see the ascent from the shadow, we need to attribute it anything we dare to give. What fear we harbour at giving un-life any credit.

The volatility it has is violent sometimes, so we tread carefully, but always the loopholes it has catch us.

With definite certainty I am suffering some blackness that I have yet to discover in myself.

For the meantime I will find comfort in it, while it teaches me its lessons.

I think I'm bound to it – yet the wielding of it is the key.

Miners must have a good grip on it, living the rise from darkness so often. If I were to move underground, I would need strong philosophy to survive – it reminds me of wanting to be nocturnal. What would I accept then?

A feeling of even greater appraisal of what the next thing is that has sprung from the abyss... Am I too much of what I am? Like a vampire? Somehow just an abortion of what should have been.

Is not the norm that we believe that at the beginning everything was blank; and we associate that with the promise or opportunity of being?

All I can say is that for some reason, it's the opposite for me. My eye sees and creates in my brain from not white or colour but from black. Straightening the line from black to white.

Does it make a circle where all the colour is squashed into a quarter with white at the top, black at the bottom and grey on the left or right? I don't know how to assign proportions accordingly, yet the shadow is as highly regarded as its opposite...

Spiritual Blackness

I contort in this body, for reasons unknown this movement is part of what I live for. Unable to divide myself from the nurturing feeling of becoming better, I train myself every single day. Just moving through it is all I want.

Every inch is so worth it. Only my former self feels the pain that is the pressure I do not escape from ever. This being ahead of it – an unquenchable yearning that drives me further and further...

Spirals that I have no control over pave my way through the aether, each step the incorrect one, yet just SO invigorating. I know I am doing right by myself – everything feels wrong, but that is what I have gotten used to. The frontrunner in my own life – always facing the darkness of unknowing and potential despair.

Will this finally be the way? Is this what living is like? Somehow foiled and made at every moment. Becoming whole and breaking at the same time – this ever-manifesting golem that births itself into reality in the face of all that oppose.

What am I really? This beacon that resonates power along with unknowing. Undefinable and yet acceptable, for there is no other way to survive.

Not understanding how this movement can make it, logic tends to predict an ending, yet we are consumed with new beginnings at every turn. The retreat yields nothing but depression and disappointment – so it is discarded again and again. What do we escape to?

Sturdiness is built like bone; some beings break it intentionally for stronger growth. This seems to be what I am doing – somehow unsatisfied with the feeling of having let go.

Dragging the lower versions of myself into a higher state I do not get enough – I forgo the need for saviour from what I am. By no chance at all I make it here again and wreathe in the too familiar boredom. This just cannot be it. Not for real – having to live with my failures. It's such a chore weeding through lesser perceptions. I wish to just let go, shatter, or sheer them all at once, so that I may find release. Yet I do a bad job of nipping it in the bud always.

Lacking in spiritual proficiency some things need to be accepted and then worked through diligently.

This knowledge that restarts a myriad of cycles I just don't want to escape anymore.

As I break the abyss that is self-created, inadequacy falls onto my base and mixes the muck. Droplets splash my face and heart – the pitch being a sticky substance that meshes into the matrix that is my being.

The shadow I will always cast is just a part of me – it's not all of me.

Black v4.0

As I put on the darkness I feel at ease, somehow clothing myself in something fitting. Expressing the myriad of interpretation I have for the shade, there is that addicted notion of being a slave to the negative.

I see it everywhere and it fills me with a warmth I cannot describe. It's like I've put on the burn that nurtures my soul – that armour I wear that cuts into my skin, yet makes me willing to fight.

When I think of respect it has to be black somewhere – without it you don't get mine.

The awareness of it just puts me at ease, cool, you're also in harmony with your shadow.

"Where is the dirt that creates your character?" I often ask people, in my head. How does one live without it, what's there to love?

For this reason, there is pride for me – it's like a "look what I have conquered" costume.

It's everywhere my eyes cannot see and taints what my eyes can. So why must I live with an averting gaze toward something that sticks out a mile? There is pain when I think of the shade, like a thud it irritates intermittently. This sensation is one I am not immune to yet.

The rest of the dark has formed part of me and it's like I seek it in my world. Do we need chaos and despair, or is it yet another thing we choose to escape from? It must be an art of handling extremes – as a level becomes too much to bear we choose another path…

I guess what I am attempting to express is a distaste for the resentment black has gotten – be polite to your teachers you learn in school.

The beatings never end, but do you do the damage before you go to sleep, or does the beating become you?

I prefer doing damage – it's good for my self-esteem. This way I know when I have fought and when it's time to call the ceasefire. It yields relaxation, atonement, and content – sometimes even pride.

Of course, there is no ongoing war, but life has a way of summoning you the moment you're ready.

The maelstrom.

Metallic Black

This sleek construct births ideas of what is cool – shining when put into the right angle, we know this is unique in some form or another.

There are so many finishes; and they all invoke fear, danger, and respect. No softies use this shade – we mean business. And mean business it is.

Guns and studs along with dark cars and crow bars, open doors to serious parts of life. Painters that use this colour must feel as though they are contributing to the evil in the world.

For we do not attribute gloss or shine to anything we do not cherish.

There is enticing detail to something metallic – a complement if you will. The epidemic on top of an epidemic. Somehow reminding of dark matter, absence yet something – the celebration of nothing or is it the celebration of the dark? It's more than that – it's the holding high of that which we hold dear. Be it respect, or mystery, others' fear of us, making a statement, or secrecy, the night or even glimmer it gives before it fades when the moon is out.

The reasoning is almost futile when it comes to black – it symbolizes the void and that is truly what most of it is. Indescribable in some ways, and only failing at giving it purpose. It lives on its own, without our help, and it shall continue to do so. Perpetuating itself due to its deep roots in all we have touched – philosophy cannot even touch it at times, because it escapes grasp.

The fact that it shimmers is like giving life to something dead, a reanimation. As darkness always resurfaces so it will use the tools that fit to it. Black on black like an assassin. It's deep beauty will be known of forevermore – deemed the negative, what we fight against. Yet do we truly win in the end?

Somehow, a part of us always turns into it before we can stop it, and so the residue leaves us panting like dogs. There is damage when confronting darkness – especially when it even makes itself noticed through accentuation. It's versatile between being welcoming, deceitful, sly, often just in your face and it bears secrets – you just don't know anything about it.

It's the bullet holes in the mind – that which no one sees. Hiding in plain sight, yet you will not grasp it.

Try as you make a fool of yourself, black will just stay above you.

Grey

Between nowhere and somewhere this shade holds mystery. Seemingly capable of holding the reverence of colour and the lacks thereof within its grasp, we can associate anything logically possible.

A matt finish results every time as our eyes perceive a numbing sensation that dull blades also deliver.

A time of dawn holds grey in its grasp or the sadness of winter. Often weather will not know what colour it wants to display and settle for grey. Not really black and so far from white we need merely a tint, and we get here – where extremes meet to form something our minds do not understand.

The wonder is in ambiguity – letting it in with that sense of being a middle of things. Not quite either way, not there yet and not becoming. Just fine with bad circumstances and just fine with good circumstances.

We won't know what will be and we do know what is not.

How I wish I could change into my opposite... But there is no such possibility. I am what I am – my counterpart the splendid use of colour in its massive variety of forms. So brimfull of possibility that it's overflowing – bursting. So here I am, unappreciated – incapable of being so and yet humble enough to accept that I do not birth anything special – nor do I work to any detriment.

For some reason I am a cornerstone, yet the unsung one. Hype is missing, while no one fears coming my way, for I am

OK.

Not at your fingertips and not miles away, I will stay at the edge of your consciousness while you decipher me one day at a time – please use my easing qualities when you find them necessary, I am soft and kind to the touch.

The times when you are in fog you will know of me but getting to know me is impossible. I sway in the wind and mesh with light air as you mix me into white and black at your disposal. Know that I need a lot of cheering up and nearly anything upsets me. Be polite, for that is what I show you – I merely want to be treated the same way I treat you.

We all have our faults, so be aware of your good sides and play to your strengths while you let them overcome your dark side. You will come to see that a droplet of anger will darken you impeccably and the work you churn into yourself will brighten your quality of life significantly.

So do not be shy of working hard – with respect for recipe you get out what you put in.

The Grey Area

Shoddy and capable of bruising, this place reminds me of a hard fall. Scratches will be felt in times to come, as gravel tears through my skin. Was I wrong to test my metal? Who was I not to endeavour beyond my capabilities – journey into the unknown and see what I can do?

Simply because it's possible I did it, but do my morals suffer too hard to keep the ball rolling?

I am certain that my stance was correct – as ambiguous as it was, my feet were planted in new soil. Does the adventurer get the prize or is prize's bounty yet another adventurer…?

We do not know until we find out, and even then; we increase the horizons perimeter.

Why do we stray from what we know? The outskirts are so daunting, yet the promise of something even better lies in wake. Like the Bermuda Triangle, we fly into darkening skies to see for real if we can truly disappear from our pasts.

Are we in search of total renewal or utmost blackness? Forever we will delve into this scenario that has us brighten at times and add scars to our old bodies at others.

There is no plan when we get there – so full of originality. The peril is worth it sometimes and we might lose some of our forces but the heroes that do survive, get fame for trying.

The means justify the end – at least the presumable one. Are we rolling the dice? It will come down to votes that prove bravery or intelligence along with trust and loyalty.

What is there to gain from another adventure into another unknown? It is the mystery we are addicted to. We won't know any time soon and hard work must ensue to create a pay-off that is worth it.

None have drawn a map for where we are going; and trouble can be at every odd step – do we risk it?

Vision is paramount in these waters, so do we lead ourselves every step of the way or do we conjure understanding of the one that anoints himself with perspective over what is to come?

Our experience and fear will have us hide away, but the fearless and brave turn our inner gaze toward treasure.

All we have is faith in ourselves – our ability to perpetuate our resolve. To sustain inadequacy and become bolder and bolder.

Push that envelope under the door – someone just might open it in your face with longing for your arrival.

Off-White

So entirely not the same, for it boasts the anti-climax that is ordinary. There is comfort in a shade that does not bear the over-the-top stature that is true white. Somewhat in its shadow, off-white is kind and forgiving in a manner of accepting; and giving a sense of feeling at home.

It is unpresumptuous and will let you feel at ease. Some crave the feeling of speciality, but this is a need we all have – fulfilled to the core when we glance upon everyday off-grandeur.

There is an absence of pressure, and we can just be – like infants in a mother's embrace we come to terms with what is natural and good for us.

The in-your-face bleakness is subsided here – not pale and empty. Full of texture and structure, the lattice forms a net of sturdiness in the mind.

For reasons unknown our heads calm down in beautiful awareness of ease.

Sometimes I've had too much, and I need to delve into excitement, yet returning is a cycle that yields greater yearning for something more vibrant.

It is as though the off-white is up-to-scratch – a staple in life. Unnoticed and not appreciated fully, it has an off-beat nature that cannot be celebrated. We would have to diminish our values for other colours to cherish off-white more and it does not want that for itself. In its rightful place we know that it should not change – for that would change us. We are fine with what we are, knowledgeable of what's good and bad – somehow knowing that this shade expresses us so delicately and without judgement.

A part of us resonates with the undertone – not wanting more, being fine with less and adhering to what is.

What more can we say when something meets expectations in all forms? There is nothing better and less is incomparable.

In its unique way I would use cream as a backdrop to my home, but is it overwhelming? So much contrast at once, and in such mass... I find that, like all things, there needs to be a middle way – a responsible use. Wildly spraying this paradox all over would result in boredom to the point of being palpable.

I choose to be mindful – enough immersion.

Whiteness

The new beginning. So much promise and trust in something new, that one cannot help but be joyous. The gaze upon a blank sheet holds such candour and love for what could be – a blank sight full of possibility.

Oh, what miracles we can create now, everything is open to the imagination and the limits are gone.

For me this poses a grudge for having to do work – no, why would I start this without the necessary preparation? How do I achieve my dreams with the presumption of greatness in mind?

There is so much pressure, that I falter. Like a butterfly emerging from a cocoon this start may mean that there is going to be strife. The creative flow will be there, yet this means I'll have to jump over obstacles and stumble over stones along the way.

I can envision the jovial within this expanse and understand the longing people have for hatching into a blank slate – as if the past no longer exists.

Forever I will be torn between my past, present and future, along with being enslaved to depicting my life onto empty paper to show what I am.

Nothing has happened yet... What good is this if I cannot be glad or sad about a story that has yet to be told? The narrative is missing and so dependent on the writer. Do I love the emptiness because it is missing exactly this? That absence of implication and expectation – somehow sensing what the storyteller is on about, going to be on about and making a point of.

Do I predict what I read or create for myself? Am I reading the same story I seek to tell a little differently each time so that I stop being bored? At least I see my own evolution, always peering ahead into the unknown. White truly scares me because it's like all of creation is involved with my new endeavour.

The world flows through me onto the blankness and I am abhorred at what I see. Must I face this reflection every time I open a new document?

Far from perceptions of what I have experienced, the value of ignorance becomes realized within me – I can unsee and forgive. Wiping it clean to try anew, fresh perceptions along with a barren landscape full of fertile soil.

My mind conjures up only what I wish to keep, and the brush will only paint what is deemed worthy – in such fashion I will sculpt my now to be at peace.

For myself, the ones I love and the rest of existence.

Pearl White

Glimmeringly it's like a laugh of happiness and content – peaceful in its way of being. In harmony with it all there is nothing it cannot be benevolent with – wearing a smile while being so.

With divinity in its behaviour, any being that has the traits this 'colour' boasts will treat you with kindness and capability. Precious and rare such armour is – fending off the needles life throws with ease and style. Elegant and pricelessly each gesture is that of a being living in self-achieved glory.

When painting this substance there is an air of gentleness and splendour to it – as if wielding silk.

The use of it will make any artwork special – anyone glancing upon it will notice that they should pay tribute to the accentuating droplets of pearl that speckle the nodes of what is meant to be perceived as grand.

Celebrating the delicate points with empathy we feel that this use is accurate and appropriate – long has one contemplated on the use of such an epidemic.

It can be used to display something that is even cute – giving rise to individuality and projecting a character to indomitable heights.

Lace becomes very fine and leaves you with a sense of respect and the responsibility to care with all you've got – please only give your utmost. For we do not show this often, peaks are displayed here – so understanding of how you should cherish is vital.

How does one return to normality after witnessing the finale that is pearl? Like a new beginning, everything before it is in shadow. Glisteningly the memory of its shine has transformed us into new creations so that our principles and expectations of life may be raised. We have seen something greater now, and we know to cherish the smaller things better.

The mundane needs to be a collection of stones that form the foundation of buildings that resound such colour unto the outside world. All we strive for is to build such greatness once again.

Even having done so once is enough to motivate us for every new task of erecting beauty that is worthy of wearing pearl white.

Often discredited due to unfathomable nature along with inability to treasure accurately, we fall short of achieving this shade consistently. Yet we try and with a little luck we sometimes succeed.

All the more reason to keep hope alive.

Silver Sliver

The apex of grey evolution, this band marks the anointment of what we hold dear. None can compare to being the underdog and succeeding to boot. Everyone is trying and silver is achieving.

Far from the infamous first place we do not care too much for praise – for it is the personal victory that counts all too much. I was on the scoreboard, and some might cherish my victory as much they value platinum more than gold.

A hint is all I ask – just see me up there among the greats. Once there it means I can do it again, maybe differently each time, while my creative confidence never suffers.

I accentuate with undertone and fittingly show what needs to be made aware of. In my nature I am just as good as any other, yet I have my own mark. Slightly lesser in some interpretations, but perfect in my own.

I get overused as chrome and misused when I have a shimmer – my underwhelming touch soothes the ones that seek appreciation in harmonic amounts and not down shall I look, but to my right and left for quality makes the podium.

Blades wear me for practicalities sake, yet the katana slices through. I finish what I start and accurate responses, along with due respect, is what I deserve.

Why is my better brother so self-absorbed and I so much the opposite? Do our values trickle into which place we achieve? For then, I am far greater! In my humbleness I stumble over vanity – is it a secret that I wish to have his place along with my own? Do I want the podium for myself or is this just the reflection of having been on it in the first place? What I mean to say is: my place is just, but why do I not know for certain where it is?

How do we determine just not good enough to be the only one and yet pay so much tribute to three?

My doppelgangers all shine so vibrantly in their myriad of hues and here I am obsessed with something that I am not. We are too different this time – and somehow, we will always be so.

In my place I am insecure but established. If you make use of me correctly; I shine yet pin me against my foes and I will fail you. It takes a clever mind to understand how I flow into reality – complementing those around me with kindness, yet resilience in my heart.

Please cherish me for what I am – the subtle compliment you've been waiting for. That silver lining.

Colours...
Foreword

To start off with; I would like to mention that even though I might at times slant things to seem like the common perception, in some of my works, I motivate you to know that the perceptions I show are merely my own. Agree, disagree, find the middle, make up your own mind, replace and admire. I believe perception can merely be shared and taken up individually as you tailor your own the same way I attempt to wield mine.

This book is meant to give a hint of fascination with colour – to lend inspiration for each and to have fun reading about a common factor we share in life. Choose what we will, we won't be divided from colours, interpretations, character traits and philosophy (to name a few) I wish to combine these topics into a display or glimpse at colours that I love writing about.

Being an artist myself, I am obsessed with delving into specific 'energies' and yielding the mental results. Being in love with describing things, it gives me much pleasure to outline my view on the myriad of colour. Here are the ones I could muster the courage to write about. I hope you enjoy!

Light Blue

This colour makes me think: "It's a boy!!!" Comforting notions of the whole family getting knowledge of your joy that is growing in the wife's tummy.

Many days of playing with 3D-printed aeroplane and cars or even rockets and stars will be lived in proud wonder at a miracle of life. Being a dad must be a daunting but fulfilling task, and one that not every man can undertake. I presume it takes a lot of confidence to lead as the main example of someone that will know you his entire life.

Furthermore, light blue reminds me of the smoke some planes leave behind in the sky – like advertising for how awesome airspace is we find these signs in thin clouds when the weather is right.

There is an air of openness and delicate freedom if seen with a keen eye.

Not much of it, but it is there – like something that needs to be nurtured to bloom. The hue is faint and temporary, for big spaces cannot be covered in it for long. Having the sense of getting boring pretty quickly, light blue has a subtle joyfulness to it that is fleeting.

Returning to your child that is rapidly becoming a man we see that other colours seem to switch places with light blue.

Once I painted with this hue, I was amazed, but today I could not be more bored. Its pale and uneventful nature needs to be stimulated by the addition or contrast of other colours. Using it as an accentuate is very nifty and wow, does it shine brightly when used sparsely.

Having the traits of silver and few other colours that resound when made use of in small quantities it works well on the mind – lending relief and a sliver of gentleness.

Aero

This hue seeks to remind us of the effortless nature that seagulls experience in summertime…

How gracious nature is with its ability to produce livingscapes that birth openness of the mind, body, and soul. The feeling of air rushing past the face, feathers or body must be enlightening and freeing.

Aero has within its name this light affect, like a breath of fresh air. My mind conjures up images of fluffy clouds and slipstreams that must be wonderful to traverse.

Being a shade of blue; it lets me think of a refreshing breeze over the shore as waves crash against the smooth stone to form this uplifting spray of water.

Aeroplanes have the style of aero within them and it is no miracle that cars were fashioned to liken them back in history as this streamlined feel has a sleek and elegant sense.

There is something modern about a form that is so much accustomed to this invisible faction within existence. As if combining technology with physics and the mastery of manipulation of this element.

The effect of modern techno-culture meeting the pinnacle of science and manufacturing ability is one that lends confidence and trust in our ability to shape our future. The dawn of the electronic car and maglev trains have the same air of professionalism that makes us proud to live in this time. We do not want to live as the Jetsons, but we don't want to let go of our past either, so the middle way is great for now.

Our children's children will live in what we can only call utopia, where our motor vehicles run off of the vapour gathered from spires clad in foliage. By that time, we will have said goodbye to small towns in the mountains that are nearly self-sufficient, and we will have said hello to a globalized culture that is bent on working together like the well-oiled machine it is meant to be.

Hinting at us still choosing simple lives over the too modern, hectic lifestyle – I see us overcoming stress with clever easing of workflows and the meticulous use of spreading the load onto the entire workforce, so that we no longer rely on so very few to do the bulk of the work when it comes to areas that only specialists can handle.

Of course, my head is in the clouds, but these can only be hopes and dreams for what I wish to experience in my life still. We cannot know how far we will go, yet recognizing our explosive rises in the recent one hundred years I do not see us slowing down at all.

Success favours the diligent and that is surely something we are…

Losing my head in the wind, I think this colour would fit with off-white in artwork of nature that can contrast its opaqueness with clarity and fine linesman ship. Good in big spaces for its mind-clearing quality or used in tiny specks to accentuate stars in the sky. It has some versatility if you put your mind to it – for air is everywhere.

Faded and Washed Blue

Like the trails of cigarette smoke there are spirals and patterns that stimulate creative growth in the mind, yielding new energy to being interested in how calmness can be expressed.

In my life I often am forced to glance at slate that layers a surface with the cracked cement at its edges.

In a dance, the natural flow reminds me of how nature operates – a seemingly random collaboration of forces that provide me with inspiration to continue portraying the endless nuances of reality in as many forms as I can.

There is an infinite quality to this hue that speaks of intricate detail, while having a worn effect that shows the way time erodes parts of us while rebuilding what we put our thoughts to.

I find this in blue because water has an unstoppable flow that etches its marks slowly with an unseen hand. How many rivers have been carved and crevices cut through the unending torrent that is the will of water?

So, we are formed and fashioned through our times in life that we may wear tiny scars that are the wrinkles in our skin. When we are young; we make the first folds and bear them in our youth all the way to our demise – where they have become us.

This hue, if one can call it that, is the example of true wisdom that has come into contact with the harmony of flow. Of course, there will be many different interpretations, yet I find that much like staring at the horizon when at the sea, this wash gives rise to thinking with wonder – a timeless space that is at peace with clouds dissolving into near nothingness and infinite expanses eventually boasting peaks and troughs.

So, the etchings in the stones I see must be for the ants that traverse the planes they provide for them – each step down or upward a new level of terrain. I am fascinated with what my eyes behold and the affect it has on my brain – recreating notions of where things start and end and how the patterns elongate and diminish in such a swerving, a true-to-itself nature.

My head wants to go on, but it has an air of getting lost in such massive space. Zooming in and out is a fun act but the lines get blurry – I don't want that to happen.

Else I would end up faded and washed – like the blue that I view.

Sparkling Blue!

My eyes are blinded by the shimmer that is the reflecting and swaying of water at pools of calm enlightenment. How ever-changing a surface can be in its natural way when stirred or agitated. It produces patterns that glisten in optimistic playfulness and the mind feels enthusiasm in sprites.

To achieve a conscience as clear as a pond's, which stays translucent while retaining that still-blue even when a pebble is thrown into its centre – that is the goal some beings wish to achieve.

The question is how to refine one's touch on the mind in such a way that we do not create crashing waves – instead, create bubbles and ripples that caress and compliment.

How do we assess our own states in wholeness, and can we ever experience ourselves in our entirety? Does the mind even have the capability to fathom what we are as each moment changes us into yet another upgraded form?

Far in the future we will have meditated until our backbones are stiff and we wield energy to such lengths that we create orbs of light with our hands to usher in ages of might and magic.

In my imagination I hope that in a life ahead I get to launch ice lances and electrify electric eels with the same sort of bolts Zeus used to stifle the ones that were against him.

In how many games do we create from our minds, hope, and wish that it could be true – while what is birthed in the mind eventually sees the light? All too often I notice when a thought has reached fruition and I utter it – in speech, in writing and in the rest of the art I dabble in.

Is it too much to hope for magic to be real? We cannot put a finger on it; but we believe in true love, destinies, certain occurrences being meant to happen, walking a path set in stone by ourselves at every moment and reality only being capable of functioning in terms of our collective imagination. So, what if we changed that?

Of course, I am joking but the wish was there! Maybe we will discover new ways of seeing the world through our children's children. Maybe beyond our current perception lies a world that we can only now form with our heads for it to become real!

If only it were that simple... We have to factor in our understanding of the material plane as well as the unknown world of the spirit along with how projections of the future impact time now, and so the list of reasoning for incalculable odds goes on...

But here's to dreaming! When I die; I want to herd unicorns for my princess bride and fight dragons! I wish to cast a snowstorm onto the village somewhere in elf land that laughed at one of my stories.

I dream big and it's fun!

I'm not being serious, but my point is that the mind is a playground that is nearly untouched at any given moment – what is stopping us from having some joy while we think? So much seriousness in the world and we can't seem to catch a breath and laugh at what a bounty the world of unseriousness has to offer!

The boundaries are all in feels and knowing someone – now you know this side of me, giggle away ☺

Cyan

Carefully resonating a thick energy this colour lets me feel at ease, sprinkling joy into my conscience. Nuances I get from having played a computer game that uses this hue often make me think of time well spent. As if I had purchased hours of good experience, I sailed across skies and my ears basked in calming electronic music that hummed and sparkled sprites of deep, melodic and enlightening tones.

If I would think of a spirit bathed in this colour, I would imagine a soft light centre emanating cyan in a harmonic fashion. In tune with the world, itself, and its immediate company – it must be wonderful being around a person that has traits in this hue.

I would get too much of it eventually, being filled with passive unwinding into a utopic mindset that is so divided from reality that I can only think of robots that would create such a living space.

Found on the edge of the horizon at times and seen in futuristic scenes, cyan has a cool name and a nice spelling – I love z's and y's. They're special.

Thinking of a lot of opaque surfaces I could put this on, it lends itself to expanses depicting holidays and cocktails. White beaches with translucent waters at their edges.

Fish often bare this shade of blue, emulating the waters they call home to add to the array of vibrant life such places hold.

Free from negatives I perceive cyan – to me, synonymous with clever notes in electronic music that boasts the feelings of the tropics combined with peaceful, intelligent city life.

How I love to take a break and escape to such destinations – because of such, to some elevator music I am glad that I invested in wireless headphones so I can elegantly dance in privacy to the rhythm that is in the ambience.

It almost becomes a private affair until I turn up the volume and the beat takes over. Pulses would go through my body as the energy I attribute to the visualization of this hue becomes an experience on its own. It is because of such things that I believe in the word 'energy' so much – it is versatile and different every time, yet somehow it resonates differently at times and when shared with people.

The English language needs to come up with a more intricate description, or maybe I should read through an entire dictionary at some point. Yet I feel as though it is more the delving into the word itself along with mental pictures drawn around it that make the difference.

At least I hope this depiction did not disappoint, for else I would have the pleasure of rewriting cyan and go through this space once again.

Zima Blue

How I have longed to see such art – my life can be categorized into before and after seeing this episode of Love, Death & Robots.

Before, I sought something that would show a primal form of the spirit and afterward, I felt this need to be quenched.

On display is a story of what we all seek; an inhuman act that we all wish we could achieve – would the world not be a better place without the pressure of needing more? How much does it take to become still in oneself…?

Having spent countless hours in meditation I have yet to be completely at peace with where I am going, because I cannot see. It is far too mysterious, what life may bring – the impulses I have to spontaneously do things that I feel I am driven to do, through sheer lack of not settling for less.

Are we at the whim of opportunity so often that we cannot withstand temptation? How long does it take until the temptation of inner peace supersedes the will for trivial things such as success…?

Being caught in a drive to finally reach some place – maybe then I'll be fine, maybe then…

So often I hear and read that you arrive by knowing that you are already there. I do not skip ahead and think in terms of things being manifest already yet seek to be in harmony with the now. I find it presumptuous to prance within the knowing of my destiny and suffer at the feeling of living in the past. I think

I am deciphering what thoughts feel like when they're present. But am I trying to distil instant manifestation? Is this too much to be capable of? At its mere least I do not know if it's even possible...

Having seen a cycle end, it lets me know there is always hope. In the endless flux we turn and twist in ways that satisfy every moment – in a tunnel that is past, present, and future.

Remembering a part of the episode I liken the scene of where one of the main characters compares the blue – times are like this: one cannot really make out when what is. We pull future and past into the present and to spite us, this affect makes them pull the present into past and future – so what is time really?

Azure

This hue has a philosophically romantic vibe to me because I picture my mind floating above the drama in a pristine manner, like a dragon to crisp and intimate electronic music.

It conjures up grand images of a blue ice dragon that could breathe its chilling torrent of frost on whomever may disturb its peaceful nature. Scales glistening in the nearly cloudless sky as the sun reveals their strength – almost gem-like and sturdy. Majestic beings dragons must be, and I so hope they exist somewhere! Not to be hunted but adorned for their resilience and beauty. They must be the culmination of aeons worth of evolution! Nature producing something that stands tall against the biggest foe – humanity.

The air of electronic music comes from so many tunes I have heard that brighten my heart's radiance whenever my ears are calm enough to take in such subtle, yet powerful energy. The fact that the music has electricity running through its metaphorical circuits means to me that it is otherworldly in nature, like the dragons. Nearly birthed from the magic that is in imagination it creates a feeling of freedom and peace within that tough right to defend itself.

As if having risen above strife and comfortable in its own skin it's made itself known and respected; and that is something worth cherishing.

To paint an even greater picture – I see endless mountains protruding into the open as far as my eye can see. Each turning a deeper shade of azure as they fade into the horizon. The dragon could be in the front, waiting for its mates that are flying and the closer one might be ready to land.

Maybe I have read too many fictional stories, but the idea I have in my mind of dragons is one of a misunderstood creature that had to fight its way into peace. So happy and comfortable there where the ocean that is sky and mountains kiss. Simply the idea of being a dragon rider is a mind-blowing thought.

It would combine the love of nature with a relationship to a being so powerful, while being vulnerable at circumstance. A being that opens up to very few who have opposed it in the past. It offers the opportunity to make things right...

Greater than birds, the scales from fish and the colour of another world – the mental image I have created for you will always be in my mind and now I am glad you have it too.

Aquamarine

This extremely beautiful hue is boasted by the gems that wear it so proudly. It brings me a joy that seems to spring eternal from the basis – such jubilance and splendour. I would drench a bathroom in this 'shade' of turquoise if I were an interior architect and live in it until my dying end.

In my old age it would revitalize me and during my stay with such exuberance I would rejoice every morning after washing my face.

It's like waking up to something miraculous!

Furthermore, it combines the two words aqua and marine. Aqua might possibly be my favourite word and I shall go into detail soon, but marine has such a natural tone.

Everything connected to marine life gives me the sense of being pure and in balance – as if we have so much to learn from the ocean.

Down there it's like space but aqueous – closer to our imagination and some adventurers can even travel there.

My trips snorkelling and watching lionfish from the surface along with engulfing adventures in aquariums that have an open passageway have left me bedazzled at marine life. Tales of Atlantis spring to mind as I could envision myself as a member of the team that goes there.

How beautiful an experience it must be to broaden the horizon of mankind with each step into a new world. Like the daunting task of being an astronaut, yet a tad safer.

Aqua – the name in itself has wonder about it and when I have fluent thoughts it reminds me of flowing water that I am pondering. Ponds! They contain aqua and the nature in its ecosystems is just as gorgeous as that of the marine. Colourful frogs and dragonflies that sit on waterlilies strewn in breathtaking arrangements in parks and gardens.

Not to forget the intricate knowledge of balance that water implies; it has many symbols rooted in equilibrium to efficiency. To me the list goes on and it is no wonder that aqua is the first of a human's three basic needs…

Powder Blue

Fresh from the spray booth this hue has a shimmering effect that puts a smile on any fanatic's face. Be it on an aeroplane, car, or lamp stand. It awakens something spritely within us and bedazzles.

Its airy sense of being makes us light-hearted and happy while reminding of a better place in time when life is exciting and new. Like a thrill it pulls up the corners of a mouth to make dimples appear.

Jubilant but serious it has a fine touch of a master and stylish while easy-going pizazz.

We are drawn to making things chromatic and powder blue makes it sparkle even harder. I have seen so many car shows in which artists could not help themselves but make them powder blue for its modern elegance.

The colour of the young and vigorous any old-timer could relive the days of his youth.

If I were to be bold, I would fashion jewellery in this hue and make a shocker out of a red dress for my wife once she has all the sapphires she can wear, to fit with this.

Contrasts work wonders, I think. Otherwise, a nice white and chrome would do the trick. Good for big surfaces and brilliant at intermediate fades this works as a good eye-catcher if you let it shine.

It has a flashy sense to it and draws a lot of attention, so stay away if you want something delicate.

Brilliant in the show-offs' eyes and it's good to rely on if you want to make a consistent impact on who you are attempting to impress. The go-to colour for proper and sustainable 'wows'.

I cannot help myself praising this shade, for its effortless coolness is unlike any other. If I were into painting surfaces a solid colour; then this would be it. There is no parallel except timeless classics that just seem monotonous in comparison.

It reminds of peace out at sea, the wind in the heavens and fluorescent birds in the jungle – so where can you go wrong?

Dark Blue

This hue lets me think of the deep sea – far below the surface where it's happy I feel knowing of sinister creatures like grey krakens and the angler fish that lures its prey into its gritty maw with the promise of light.

Almost evil such depths are for they synergize with what we do not know of, yet within this unknowing we birth dreams of beautiful reality such as the myth of Atlantis, but also regrettably the horrors such as the story of Cthulhu.

Holding close the notion of uncharted-ness, the use of this colour promises mystery and anguish – a longing to know what's out there, much like staring at space as the sun goes down or a picture of earth from orbit.

We want to know, but this quality is infinite – we can only fill our minds with what's interesting to us and there is simply too much. We are overwhelmed with drives to find, search, discover and unearth – so much so that we send expeditions into the utmost corners of reality, only to find that we are already OK with what we have in the end.

How much more can we take before we develop a balance between seeking and resting in contentment?

I fear and hope the adventure never ends as day by day I find new inspiration and conquer old habits that see me blossom into new forms of expression and reverence for the deep blue.

I have a pair of jeans that I feel proud to wear because it displays a sense of peace with unknowing – not quite there yet, but eventually putting dark blue into its place, the fear of it will subside and I shall grow bored of pinning yet another sliver of angst onto the mural of my conscience.

This hue has no hope of being joyful and does not promise any feelings of spontaneity or enthusiasm. Instead it provides us with existential crises and inferiority complexes that stem from being part of the ocean in its vastness yet being the ocean in a drop.

Philosophically I have never felt a greater tear at my being than from this likening – it is nearly unfathomable but delivers power and confidence.

Like the angler fish's prey, I have become a victim of this phrase and I do not know when I will be able to understand it.

Phlox

This shade of purple has a resonance to it that shines out happiness in a humble, cute, and subtle way. There are flowers named phlox and they are as delicate as most flowers are with a mischievous kindness about them.

To me it's as though they trump sadness and bitterness with the joy of abundance and innocence.

How do I see so much in a mere flower you ask? It is a matter of going inside the soul and revealing what you see in yourself when you look at such beauty. This act of meditation is one that one gets used to when spending a lot of time solitarily.

I have cultivated this practice to learn about life – to see the light in the dark no matter how dim I shine. It is this trait that lets me appreciate a small flower which is colloquially known as the phloxie as if it were as great as Mount Everest.

So, we find things to be grateful for when times get tough, so that we have motivation for each new day.

I think it a common thing that has lost its value over time due to routine and other habitual preferences regarding views of individuals that do not practice mindfulness so diligently because they do not simply have the time.

We live in a fast-paced world where everything has to run as best as it can – this makes us not cherish relaxation and work on self or even time in nature as much as some cultures do.

The phloxie reminds me to be patient with myself and my dreams, along with the people that mean the most to me. Even everyone beyond that deserves consideration and understanding, even though it might not always be so readily available.

Getting back to the hue: I, for one, would prefer this in special places that need the accentuation. Not suitable for medium spaces it has an all-or-nothing effect, especially well-paired with white to profit from the cute effect.

A controversial pairing would be with a yellow if you want shocking, yet elegant blues would do the trick if you want the opposite.

I am not much of a sculptor, but I could see this in a daunting abstract. Houses should not be painted this shade unless they're romantic getaways. Furthermore, I think this hue is fine in the garden where it has a nice place within nature for me; yet do go wild and have fun – it's one thing that colours are about!

Twilight Lavender

Mysterious this colour strikes me. It has a touch that makes me want to think of magnificence, yet it does not want to be named something it itself is in a haze about.

It has secrets to be found and it gives me that tantalizing notion of wanting to find out more. As if it were a treasure trove for the ones that seek that which is at the edge of their knowing.

The next step somehow, but a step into murky waters that might just be better than expected.

Luring it has a grasp on me that is enticing, yet not too much to overpower my lust for that which might be inside twilight lavender.

I can see goddesses bathing in tubs that wear this hue, petals strewn on the water's surface and maidens tending to her in the privacy of a feminine practice of taking care of the one they adorn.

Heroes would give twilight lavender to this goddess on special occasions, paying tribute to her beauty and elegance.

It makes me want to delve into fantasy so far that I could read texts on such deities if they exist in the modern novels we have. If only I could find them...

I think that is what this colour does to me – it makes me want to search for more than I am currently in.

Even dangerous to venture beyond yet enticing.

I could see this in clothing, like a dress or a tie to portrait a soothing tone. Beyond wearing the colour, I would paint it in huge ways, to display extravagance and wonder. For it is powerful.

Not being suitable for specks of it, I think medium to big surfaces it does well in; and it gives me a sense of wanting to be adored. So do it justice, but do not play with it – it has a serious touch.

Eminence

A supreme colour that radiates ability to handle life in a respectful, ordered and cultivated manner.

It invokes deep respect for the nearly divine, without overattributing it to them, yet when paired with the whiteness of this trait it shines gracefully and with peace.

I almost naturally want to bow my head to eminence and adorn those that seek to wear such quality in their spirit. It reminds me of the wise that have indoctrinated a higher culture into themselves and seek to better the world through wholehearted gestured that are subtle, gentle, and kind.

I think few in this world can truly walk in eminence for we are bound to not being used to such creatures. Almost alien, these purple beings give me the sense of floating above the ground with elegance from another world.

Too easily are our feeble minds drawn to discreditation and distraction due to vanity and jealousy.

We are not used to living with such grace and can only stand in awe and service of such powerful peace.

Yet there are eminent people in this world who have gotten there by mastering combat the royal way. Cleanly structured violence is carefully subdued, and equilibriums are reached where the opposition is made harmless.

Simply to breach on such topics makes talking about eminence a tricky conundrum. Are we discussing eminence in its various forms, or is there just the holy way? Any way you could go about it keeps functional systems in place and seeks to provide freedom of spirit. So that we can build new bridges into a greater wholeness.

Woes that I find to trouble the eminent is a tendency to be pompous – I think it has to do with realism, equality, self-preservation and self-esteem. It implies supremacy which invokes disrespect – the truly eminent can handle this inability to appreciate in exactly the manner that eminence is presented with compassion and benevolence.

If I had to choose between pairing this colour with some others, I would go with black to give the sense of understanding the negative and how to wield it, white to combine it with the greater good, or a full red to give it more love to tend to so wonderfully.

Not an easy colour to work with for you are extending the image of the royals with your hands... lots of responsibility weighs on your shoulders so be sure to compliment with candour and a full heart.

Neon Pink!

As apparent as spray paint on lockers and power boxes, neon hearts are the symbol worn by this hue – unapologetic and unhumble this force is meant to be known of and undeniable.

This colour, adhering stickily to black and white checkerboards, reminds of plastic and neo-comics read by teenage girls that wear ponytails to keep the long hair out of their faces and have their ears pierced high up.

Tattoos gotten all too soon on ankles and forearms, this style boasts punk rock and a generation that is potent and driven to prance in creative love that makes a statement.

Ineffably feminine this colour is theirs to rule from – classifying and depicting with clear judgement what is deemed cool enough and what is rejected. For females have a cut off, or nip-it-in-the-bud mentality that assesses worthiness in a primal fashion, incalculable by logic and mostly determined by vibe.

Heavy guitars and ecstatic vocals chant along the movement of this faction of activism – not bolstering weapons but a scintillating taste for life and the making of great examples for followers to enact.

It speaks to the core of being – are you with the colourful movement or simply part of the crowd that hampers on along, raising a fist in support due to fear of not following the doctrine of peer pressure?

We want spirit! Incorruptible stance that celebrates femme! These women are the new prize, for their view is open and creative – fresh but resilient. Like toy figurines of heroines we buy readily to soothe our needs for physical idols, I want one in flesh and blood.

I want to wake up with her hair in my face and fight with her to see how strong she really is.

An unyielding geist that does not submit! We do not settle for mere lazy perceptions that are not in harmony with love. For reasons unknown, our most prized philosophy will find its way into the heart of the world, even if we have to scream it from stages, collect every black unicorn and wear psychedelic clothing on our off days!

Laughter at sheepish mentalities is like a cherry on top when I imagine good times at festivals where art is displayed, and we all rock out to our favourite bands. It's a whole other movement of living, somehow just alive at the centre, just NOT asleep, NOT lulled into materialistic things, but fascinated by the experiences this waking dream has to offer.

Cheers to the little girls that picked up plastic microphones and sang their hearts out, cheers to the ones that found true love in cool places and raise your glasses to the girls that nearly always had an important message drawn on the back of their hands in schools that promoted conformity to old norms.

We made the difference by being the difference!

Light Pink

When it's a baby girl we all melt. What has the world done to receive a little angel like this, and yet another one?

Among all women, somehow when they're young they bear the same promise of becoming princesses that love rainbows and love unicorns. At least these are some of the notions I get when I think of them.

Mum's having a good time sowing dresses and reading to their daughters are some of the thoughts that come to mind, others are tattoos and bad boyfriends.

Only being capable of giving you the masculine perspective that I would have as a father, would presume a distance of misunderstanding and judgement.

To make matters better I must say: "I wish for days where I buy her sugar candy and take her on rollercoaster rides while mum takes care of the 'owchies' the boys inflict."

I cannot imagine life being very easy when raising a little lady in this day and age, yet what does all of this have to do with light pink?

Beyond being the girly colour, to me it resonates with women in general – I have friends that will always want their memories having such a hue because it reminds them of better times.

Light pink is innocent, and that tends to be what we see in tiny females. Girls that will become quirky young women that find men their fathers hopefully approve of. So, the colour gains somewhat of a feminine touch that men cannot stand in mass. Too much is just too much, so use this hue when expressing subtle love and showing kindness.

There are so many delicate colours to choose from, but when you choose this one you better be sincere.

There is no hardness in this colour for it sees that as utterly rude – only heartfelt compassion is allowed.

Faded Pink

Creatively I think we are all buying and selling perceptions – we study to refine them, and much is spent on acquiring some that hold weight. Whether it be a renowned painting or the professional opinion of a therapist, it is something worth striving for, worth living for and worth paying for.

Connecting something faded with this topic I find that it becomes a blur when we attempt to decipher how much we actually enlisted in this process. It's pink because it has to do with love – ineffably we are sharing of ourselves, giving self-love, and assessing with a self-created opinion.

Monetarily it can be seen as an exchange, but I think the topic goes deeper: we cultivate opinion every day, to share it every day. What is our view worth when calibrating it? A sculptor would put a price tag on a piece and say: the perception this delivers is worth this much to me, so I'll charge a comparable price. The same is true for psychiatrists, doctors, architects and so the list inevitably and endlessly goes on. Even criminals share perceptions that make people fear them – I bet fear is very expensive!

Faded also gives the hint of having a wash – natural, but uncontrollable. We do not know where the lines end or begin and the net of sharing goes beyond and deep within.

If I think something to myself – is this sharing something special with myself? There is no point in a thought that does not hit its mark and so even the ones we have privately hit theirs.

Through cultivation we build view, perceptions, and opinions we eventually share with the world so that we might graduate the cycle of having had or 'created' the thought to begin with.

So, I find faded pink to be the suitable colour to describe a movement in nature that we cannot stop and yet cherish, at the other end of the spectrum, to such lengths that people make their living off of it.

So murky waters become clearer, and some become duller, yet this affect is one we live with.

Pink

This colour is great for contrasting, either to yellow or light green, in my opinion. It has that feel of being something special that also makes it have a very, very feminine quality. Men often shy away from being too pink; but we cannot seem to not like it somehow.

Within each of us is always a pink side that cannot help itself but adore the sides it brings out in us.

Like pictures of kittens, it brings up an exuberance that almost screams: "I am OK and proud of being who I am!" So unique and delicate that whatever has this colour must be protected by the others.

Having a fragile nature, I find that people that master pink have a quality that is strong and steadfast.

Easily prone to insecurity, people that see themselves as mostly pink need appreciation and recognition for who they are.

I think it is within the nature of us to want to share this deep appreciation with the one we love most in this world. Someone that is nurtured by sensitivity in the privacy of a relationship.

This is where sincerity is valued and not wasted.

All too often our efforts are not taken up the way we wish – we do not achieve that ephemeral connection with everyone.

In the case of finding that special someone that sees the utmost of you and then on top of that chooses to return gestures in kind, reminds me of the word 'namaste', which in some translations means: 'I see the divinity in you'.

While my perceptions of pink are probably still quite shallow yet having some thick roots, I think my studies into this mysterious colour have only begun.

At this time in my life, I use it much like someone would describe a garnish. Dreams of pinker reality is most of which I put into physical reality for personally I find myself still to be rather immature in this area.

So, there are different degrees of professionalism within the multitude of areas one navigates, and I, for one, am glad about the 'intro' I have to this shade.

I will continue dreaming and am confident that one day I will be trained in the art of true sincerity so that it hits home more often than not – gaining a playful wield on the subject and no longer taking things of the matter too personally.

Smitten

This astounding hue has love written all over it in a girly and cute way. Of course, the innocence of young boys being smitten is also a reality, yet the resonation comes with who they are smitten for.

I imagine happy girls with their arms open in pure joy as they see their boyfriends for dates – some hastily covering their shy red cheeks and some just winging it – wearing smitten in all openness. Proud to be in love and loving it.

I can see dreams that come to life in their twenties as the young ones craft their perfect lovers in their minds and find them later on.

Weddings that start smitten all over again and romantic dates for the ages at anniversaries.

Smitten has a timeless sense that will reoccur whenever you fail to put your walls up and luckily so.

Life will have you living anew whenever it gets the chance in small and in big ways – so be on the lookout. There is a present in every moment so do not be careless with these gifts – we only have as many as we can carry; and life is long.

Eventually we will have to sift through moments of our past and incorporate them into our future, but how many good memories can we gather before our hearts overflow? This is what smitten feels like – the heart overflow. When we simply cannot get enough of what we are living. An eternal well-spring that is birthed from just carrying on in the flow of things.

We might get carried away or get stuck along the way, but that's what lovers and family are for – we weather storms together along with the odd stumble over a rock.

Sometimes take the good with the bad and others insist on things being done properly. Doing stuff poorly is not our style and we want to enjoy our lives living them. So, make it easy for one another; forgive, be compassionate and most of all, be caring when you can – with yourself and everyone that crosses your path.

Returning to the essence of this text – we are all smitten with ourselves and others from time to time, so believe in the joy when it comes. We can't be grouchy when life is handing us strawberry sauce…

Translucent Red

This jelly-like hue gives me the sense of being a delicacy – thinking of sauces with cherry flavour on ice cream accompanied by a rose is like a dream of extravagance to me. Such flirty and tantalizing appearance this hue has, with promise of pleasure and notions of almost being erotic, all on its own.

The clarity the hints of direct desire and the slivers of where the colour gets deeper. The kisses and looks that speak volumes.

There is a necessity that drives us to make love physical and it is cultivated and churned through playful romance. Sometimes it catches us unaware and at others, we work at it with such enthusiasm and dedication.

Much like a dance, we twirl and bend in the energy – angels peering at our movements of the periods of courtship must be writing books on how faintly love existed before and how grand it later became. We view couples coming together in our lives and the TV loves telling stories that we deem unsuitable for ourselves and unfathomable when attempting to see them as 'real'.

With respect to my overactive imagination - I am a heartless romantic. Not giving myself the benefit of the doubt when it comes to lesser versions of the loves I feel and also because my heart has already been stolen by my true love. Ha ha – the cliché is obvious, but I just had to – what is life without a little fun here and there?

To return to the hue at hand, I feel inclined to say it is not delicate or subtle, but delectable and palpable. It has a sense of speaking without words that I find unique – it plays with the imagination instead of blurting out the way it feels and lets its actions do the talking.

It does not need to bargain because it has taste and the ones seeking its attention only get it when they're being interesting. A short span of concentration for the ones that are worthy and then it's back to the business that is its own vanity.

Somehow making vain look good, we seek to play along as we do with almost all our idols.

Like the hornets that bare wings of translucent red, a lover that wields his or her touch wisely, with candour and knowledgeable of the prize is irrefutably irresistible.

As we adorn the famous ones that we attribute such traits to, we wish we had one of those mental figurines in our lives. I want one for myself, and I want to be one for another.

So, I find the matches that the stars make, are subconsciously this drug for one another that the other just cannot resist.

Being the kryptonite and the love potion all at once – a dangerous love affair!

Neon Red

The in-your-face-love colour! Like the apex of vocals, you adore it as though you were putting heart stickers on the foreheads of all of who you encounter when wearing NEON red in your heart!

So much better than normal full red, we really scream the language of life through the act of unapologetically 'hearting' another.

How I wish I could stay this way for the rest of my life, yet I know I would miss out on too much.

The wheel must turn, but there is no better thing than living out something like this for what it's worth!

Too few people get to live like this; and I fear that most are looked at with a shrug in mind – a sort of wannabe hippie style that resounds being glad. "Can't touch this!" starts playing in my head.

Do we feel like we could be loved in such a way? Is it calling to us at every moment? Is it too much?

At least I know I can give it to myself and share a nuance of it writing this. How many words does it take to provide a reader with the hint of ecstasy?

For the sake of it you might put on your current favourite song, sing in the shower or rock to it on your way to work. How often do we get to share something like that with someone else and not feel self-conscious?

Neon red gives me the confidence to be the activist in my

own life, give freely when I see fit and be arrogantly in love with parts of myself when the feelings come by. I hope you feel this way sometimes – even secretly.

Stuff like this is rare.

Cardinal

This mostly deep, yet complementary and content colour is daunting to me at times. To me it has the knack for overcoming negativity with pure love. So full and proud, nothing can stop it.

Boldly going its way, it is knowledgeable of its stance and sure of itself. It knows what part to play when and does not miss a beat.

Should it come, it clobbers. We know that hearts reign supreme – so mal-confidence has no place here.

When it's go-time we know we shall succeed, so let the face-off begin and the one with the most influential plumage will be the victor.

The ladies are impressed, and men are wooed as such elegance hits the floor – dazzling in splendour and every step and gesture correct.

I find deep respect anew and the dance in my mind is breath taking. My heart flutters. My pulse rises and it's like I am falling in love again, yet differently – somewhat intimidated but flattered, I think of times where I would show off a spouse wearing cardinal – maybe with dark jewellery to boast the feeling of being above it all.

Relating to the bird a bit more, I see humour in their hairstyle, as if wearing a quirkiness that could be interpreted as full of itself yet brushing the dirt off with style. Almost mischievous.

There is an air of naughtiness and playfulness that reminds

of playing with fire a bit. You would not want to step too close for that tinge might be more than you bargained for or expected.

Not all things that have to do with love as the ultimate weapon are weak in nature. If you challenge cardinal, I am sure you will get an earful. The attitude is insurmountable.

Other complementary colours might be purple to get that royalty idea out there, or pearl to play on elegance. The only hue I would avoid would be a yellow. It might clash and come off as shrill – the extremes are just too great. Brilliance meets brilliance does not always go smoothly.

Unlike cardinal, which has a lava-like form that is still close to solid enough to scorch you if you tread nearby. Do not sing its praise too greatly for cardinal is easily embarrassed, yet it brings out its softer side that makes for delightful company every day. I am positive that the vibrance is all too well saved for dance that leave audiences in awe.

May the blood temperatures rise.

Blood Red

From our veins and arteries, we are nurtured with life-giving force that stems from the red substance that runs through our bodies in a continual cycle that only ends suddenly or is predicted for time before death.

Blood red has a gruesome affect that adds severity to any space. It makes us feel serious and tugs at the mortal coil we find ourselves in. For this reason, I suspect that paintings specifically hold a great reverence for this hue – there is a feeling delivered in this with paint. Because it's runny and so similar, the specks created by the brush alongside is like the typical splatter seen in films that depict brutal endings or slick stabs, mostly in the dark.

Almost sinister and conniving this colour can be while displaying how we envision the evil or innocent to die in tragic or fitting ways. To pay tribute to how, yet again, a hue has positive and negative traits there is not only bad in this colour – we may want characters to die in our stories when a just death is appropriate, yet blood red also resembles wine that can be sipped when in deep thought about the tale.

Like a brooding wise man would have a glass, while telling of the wisdom of life to younger individuals the hue lends itself to giving sentiment to areas that need it. Pairing well with gold – there is a holiness about it, as if separate from the rest it has its own persona that delves deep into the spirit of man.

Into the deepness love can have for another, for life –

passion that fits well to blood, the fluid that strengthens us.

The spiral goes deep down to the bedrock, and the journey is a solemn one that one takes throughout a lifetime. Always digging deeper to find more of the essence one so craves – spiritual gold that is delivered through engaging in meaningful tasks like being true to oneself or expressing perfectly.

There is a carnal force at work that runs the basis of our being and makes us live and cling to life if we ever come to needing to. I think this is why we live, and blood red expresses that simply and unequivocally in its name and dim shine. On its own it already makes a statement and when paired tastefully it gets compliments from its partners.

It has the gift of expressing pain without effort due to aeons of interpretations and gives you a feeling of respect for it once the eyes hover over.

Few hues tug on my heart in any way near to blood red and nothing invokes a feeling more primal – it hits to the core.

Pomegranate Red

With invigorating life each bursting of the fruit splashes onto my tongue. Difficult to make out what's actually tasting this energy I feel as though my entire mouth is experiencing the sensation. My mind cannot help but be injected with the enthusiasm to use this hue in a creative way!

Hints of all the ways I want to love flow through my soul, and this is how I would express them if I would be a maker of taste sensation.

As too much quickly finds its mark, I cannot take any more – the mental sphere becomes so positively upset with yearning and a dire need to express that I should not crush another one with my teeth.

Sparsely accentuated with these, a fruit salad does wonders on the off day I would eat one – giving rise to making love in euphoria and just in any way using the inspiration on artwork thereafter.

Envisioning midday on an island, I wish to be spoiled with pleasant company and a look at this rarity. To dot the deepness of what red can offer – in my view there are few that compare to this one.

It is an impulse that drives the spirit to go into joyful showing of what it can achieve at special times, somehow sharing full feelings with confidence and pride.

Best suited among a rainbow, I think this version of red deems an immaculate place in the perception of colour.

Exploding through the nervous system the mixture of sour and that sliver of sweet work wonders on my brain – it is as though inspiration and imagination run deeply through me and dreams I yearn for are quenched.

Is life a collaboration of all the dreams we have, morphed into a continuous one that sees us realizing them in part, moment by moment or do we halt each experience with our minds? Attributing ends to things with an iron fist? To me this hue fights through nuances of nails that lock things in place and mocks the acts of control and violent depiction.

Laughing at the hammers that set happenings into stone as though we have some sort of knowledge of how things REALLY are.

We know SOME things really well yet luckily our perceptions can always be surpassed.

Red

Romantic implications strewn about on the white floors of apartments in the form of rose petals and breakfasts in bed make me think of heartfelt "I love you" whispered under covers and when special circumstances have arisen.

In me such imaginations stimulate the dire need to keep working on the topic of love that forms the basis of our existence. Opening the well of red connotation; there are so many references that I could make that would pay tribute to this core.

Presumably we all shallowly believe in the dream, yet how deeply do we achieve it?

The myriad is etched and littered with detail that forms patterns that can only end up with pulses of resounding intent that drives into higher and higher expressions of this red energy.

Enthusiastically we figure out how to please ourselves and the ones around us with care of our own places and individuality. The celebration of which could be a wedding that signifies the entire acceptance of another as part of one's life and in some beliefs – of oneself.

We have a basic compulsion to share, so we need partners – teammates that accompany us on this journey that is living. What better way to do it in, than to decide upon the happy person that gets to experience you for an extended period of time. There must be someone so lucky!

For it is the most valuable thing we have – intimate time

spent with another. Like a ticking clock to a bomb, we measure our experiences and weigh where we guide our energy. Many hopes and dreams are built on love and the acquisition of the statuses that depict us as: 'in a relationship'.

It means you are special to someone and can have the comfort of feeling so with justification – "Look, I have a witness!"

Romance has an air of being a story that goes through the ups and downs of a life until death do us part. Or so at least the dream presumes at any start. Yet the moments of exuberance and ecstasy are concealed in private. I miss triumphant tales of love that shine through ages. Longing to see this in action – no movie will do.

It has to be manifest in my life and I do not want to have to recycle lovers to get there, my will states in its naivety.

I falter into the bitter notion of 'we don't always get what we want' – we get what we need!

Amber

This hue holds the secrets of lost worlds, those of you that know of its preservation qualities will know that it withstands the test of time.

It conveys a quiet elegance in some shades while boasting determination in its red form. I admire this colour for its stamina and perseverance.

In solid form it likens gems that are malleable or shapable and I am sure figurines of the sort can be found on coastal markets where they take the place of gold in high trades. A magnificent quality that makes it mysterious and gives it the sense of coming from primal times like the glorious Inka.

It lets me wonder what life would be like if we treasured beauty more than monetary worth and took everything for what the intrinsic spiritual value is. Yet we need methods to gauge and so we get the miraculous effect of a bargain here and there.

If I had the skills, I would pair something amber with almost golden stone and honey pots alongside. Maybe a mandala or something tribal like a skull that is decorated with spirals such as from Central America.

It gives me an indigenous vibe that maybe only few of us understand but are mesmerised by – like the epic road to Eldorado.

I knew a proud waitress once by this name and she showed resilience, beauty, and versatility. Seemingly capable of wielding herself in public it reminds me of a soft touch that has a point and gets things done the way they ought to be. Not failing in any way, yet candid to work on her craft.

I am sure she owns a business by now, because such quality and impetus goes a long way – that is why I feel as though amber has contentment that does not hurt its own soul.

It does not boast or claim to be better and never would it go beneath its value. Like a humble piece of a puzzle...

Orange

I like the taste (as does everyone else). To me it is the most common fruit in the catalogue. Its colour a nearly bland one that does not excite my spiritual taste that much, yet it stimulates my imagination a resounding lot.

When holding such a sphere dimpled with crevices that spray the citrus like air-freshener when folded, I often wish I could just bite into one and feel the surge in my saliva glands.

Yet I have to peel at it, removing the thick skin to get to the nitty-gritty. It is what I did to discover that this colour is a chore of reflection to me because it displays a side of me I do not know well.

I have family that loves orange, but I just seem to hate it. Beyond unsharpened lenses photographing sunsets with black shadows at the bottom edges and alcoholic drinks with this tint, I cannot find anything inside me that would speak of this hue in fashions that I would of others.

A conundrum that does not want to solve itself – I am forced to peer beyond my comfort zones into stifling notions that let me think of cocky cars and the remnants of yellow and red. Extremes that I much rather prefer to the middle that I seek.

Forever in search of balance I am posed to find out what orange holds between the resilient illumination that yellow brings and the thick vigour of red.

Somehow too meek and for no reason I find it to be unpredictable when in reality, it poses no threat. It might simply be because of this that I feel no connection. Have I stumbled onto an orange hole in my perception? For the love of my soul, I'll figure it out.

Maybe in a few days or a month or a year I'll have warmed up to it – the preface of either colour I so enjoy. Until then I'll wreathe in the unknowing of finally being OK with all the colours in the spectrum.

Do I really need this vice? I suspect it is only because I have yet to journey there that I have a fear for it.

I know that harmony is the way, so I'll tread on the path that leads me into greater realization of this shade and myself, no matter how many shades I have to face.

Life must be more of an adventure than just a journey, and this is one I am embarking on!

Peach

This rosy shade of orange is full of flavour and spunk. It has that quirky demeanour that comes with being named a peach when you're being charming with a silly touch and who is to say that peaches don't taste great?

It's a nice word to use with a smirk that implies specialness and curiosity for romantic intent while also playing with everyday jargon that is projected with that 'puh' sound.

Fun to say and charismatic – I would love to be called a peach someday.

Beyond that, the phrase 'life is peachy' can be meant sarcastically or in joy. Either way sparks interest and continues a conversation or ends it.

Endlessly we can work with our speech to produce any form of wonder in our own and other people's lives – be it in the idle thinking or a song that invokes awe and astonishment.

So, we are the wielders of language and to me somehow 'peach' is a versatile word that comes with colour.

Beautifully fading into and out of yellow we can see peach do various fades into red or pink also.

Contrasting to light blue there is a shocking but pleasant affect that it has when so combined, because both colours are somewhat underwhelming.

I could, for instance, envision a car with peach wheels and a light blue body – some chrome here and there, and drive it in California. I would however need a different dress sense.

Maybe even a cool hat.

So peach is so malleable it's almost naturally a fruitful endeavour working with it (see what I did there...?)

Apricot

A subtle colour that with its lovely name reminds of the sweet taste that has that hint of sourness. Being an orange with an infection of pink it has the attributes of being soft, gentle, and girly while also being warm, characteristically, and situationally confident when in its element. It lets me think of naughty little girls that stick out their tongue after having done something cheeky in a sort of mischievous way yet preserving their innocence through a cute self-defence.

Lace and shocking blue eyes, I imagine would make an endearing costume that displays its quirkiness and charm – pink lipstick and a yellow, smaller purse to make a dashing example of how unique an outfit can be. But that's my style of woman that wears apricot, because it lends itself to a much more subtle atmosphere.

Alice from wonderland is another reminder for me – even though she didn't wear this hue, her character of being so at one with her imagination speaks of the flowers that come to life in the field. Growing and shrinking at the bite of a biscuit – a playful way of depicting childish imagination that travels into adulthoods mysteriousness.

As you may have notice it strikes me to be rather feminine in appearance and also conveys traits like self-love and appreciation very well. Easy on the eyes a dress in this shade is not a stunner, but something worth taking the time to be around.

Lending itself to a milky or floral state, there is a lot one can play around with – so the enthusiasm you have for this colour mostly depends on how well you understand it and want to delve into the rose coloured bath of sugar coated, soft sweets that apricot is.

To use it without effort I think one needs to pair it with white and paint with elegance... yet I am sure there are many uses for it in other ways. I feel as though it's a good covering colour that does well in bigger spaces and is somehow good at taking centre stage, although it has a shy way about it.

There is speciality in it, in the sense that it knows so but does not wear it on its sleeve for all to see – the beauty is in figuring it out on your own and giving her the compliment – if it fits, she will smile and glance at you with a happy smile beneath her locks.

This hue can be opaque, vivid, stringy, clunky, and almost anything else you can imagine and still does well in appearance due its individuality of character – easily impressing (at least me) it is a daring colour that has its own scintillating charm.

Beige

This hue only just makes it into being a colour for me, due to its qualities of being a nuisance while also delivering a sense of well-being to the ones that have a taste for it.

To me it conjures up images of old Mercedes that stand in abandoned garages for they have had their best days. Like corn that will be harvested, the leaves have gotten old and it's time for something more lively.

The cream effect is not worth discrediting though, because like all the calming colours it shows a feeling of being just fine with how things are. Beige goes deeper and reminds me of classical music that is played on Sundays when we are meant to just release our souls into a space in which we are unknowing of trouble and strife.

There is an air of status with this hue that humbly celebrates the arrival of a soft dream. It gives me an effect of stirred ice cream and well mixed grout in a light colour that I cannot wait to apply. As though I had waited for this moment all my life and diligently worked at getting here.

Gently and with a white form of love this colour is used to convey wisdom, mostly gained through age, and lends confidence in greater plans. It shrugs off too much enthusiasm and candour, depicting it as naïve and adolescent.

With time comes security.

Comfortably nestled in cream there is a notion that reminds me of froth that accentuates any latte and makes something ordinary a tad more delicate and special.

This is just me, but I love pairing this shade with pink to produce an even greater sense of fadedness. To compliment the slow flow of ease and wholeness that these colours provide.

Being very subtle a good artist can make an entire painting of beige and the shades close to it – which brings me back to the Mercedes: being a strong hue on its own, it provides a great amount of uses within its parameters and births an entire taste on its own.

I imagine people get lost in it – for much like eggshell and faded dark green it has its intricate uses that span beyond my capabilities.

Faded Yellow

Shine on a white surface lets me feel this hue and gives me a sense of the light not being understood quite as much as I would like it to be.

We spend hours of our days in search of brighter perspectives on our lives and once we share them, somehow, they become innate perceptions we once had. Some of them we keep close; and they form parts of our bases as we seek to integrate what good we have churned into our spirits.

Regrettably, we cannot be all of the greatness we have thought through our toil – we would be unserious and discredited. There is no walking in the light without darkness to contrast yet having gone through so much despair, we need to be aware of this fade to know of our past, to recollect the journey.

A fade truly shows progress, giving the notion being washed into something other than its brother – the whole hue.

Personally, I find few areas to use this shade, because there is a lack of a celebratory trait in it. I do not come across feeling this way often, but when I do, faded yellow resounds in splendour. It is a circumstantial colour that reminds me of eggshell or burnt sienna, since they need to be used precisely. With impetus.

When used in contrast it lends a dosed feeling – as if not in pure awareness of circumstance. Implying the rise of the colour around it, I find it has to be used as a backdrop that shows the mundane or subtle. When used to convey the hues around it, it does a good job.

It calms view into something almost numb to me – just almost alive, yet to me something alive is REALLY alive, so there I might be skewed. I attempt to find the enthusiasm in everything but faded yellow is just that – the remnant of something that is meant to be resilient in nature.

In my best efforts I can say it is like a waiting room – comfortable but torturing once you have been there too long.

Yellow

Optimistic and radiant I see this colour as – lending knowledge and certainty. When in the dark, all I need to do is switch on the light and I feel at ease. So simple an act when I know where the button is. Gone is then the frantic search in the dimness of the moon and sometime even shadier scenarios.

Magical it is to know that rays brighten vision every day and even constantly giving life to our minds. As sunshine hits surfaces, it bounces into our eyes and illuminates our inner brains, somewhat automatically raising our perceptions and expectations of how we see past, present and future.

It is miraculous to analyse this happening in simple tasks as watching the sun come up every day. I get up early and wait for my spot to be shone upon. I have realized that before I tend to be groggy and I need my coffee, in preparation for sitting still as the warmth slowly will fill me with gladness and hope for the day. After I have had this time to myself, I can start the day – to some extent seeming like I am wasting time lounging around thinking about stuff I can do or write.

It is a tedious task being so inactive all the time and then finally letting it all out in a flurry, but it is like weathering the night before dawn – once that first ray hits I siphon more of them until I am brim-full and cannot wait to get started. So, it has become natural to me that I will marinate in what has yet to bloom and then jovially celebrate my love in the sharing of what I have studied.

To use yellow accurately we can be enthusiastic and almost bold. It is a statement on its own, yet too much of it spoils the dish. It comes down to taste, but for me a fade of yellow is better than a blatant sheet of it. More capable of being used in larger quantities it glows so brightly and enlightens the mood with an effortless accentuation. In its many hues we have fun and get creative. It fits nearly any form well, meaning that if you should paint a straight line; it would shine just as brightly as when you give rise to making a crooked one seem more special.

In my experience few artworks do not benefit from some yellow, mixed in or dotted somewhere as a garnish. When really going the mile, I would complement it opposingly with purple – to really get some strong points across. As always though, art is a display of taste, and whatever yours may be, if you choose to add some light it could go a long way.

It is a warm colour used to decide the 'temperature' of a hue, so be mindful where you lessen or emphasize. Yet know that the philosophical properties go a very long way.

Thick Yellow

Much like any colour in oil it delivers something smeary but solid when dry. The creativity never ends, because so much can be done with it – the texture is so fine and malleable. Thick yellow reminds me of happy mornings where the egg yolk runs onto my plate after biting into my toast. Something so full and showing of its fullness.

Few colours have the quality of showing off in small quantities – just a hint of this and things have changed.

Nature paints with this hue over and over again to bring out the joy in life, be it on bees, butterflies, birds or sunflowers. An intricate net is cast between these examples that invokes a sense of a higher mood. A passive greater wellbeing.

As if having achieved a certain point in life that is displayed with thick yellow.

Providing a great paradox to other colours it might seem like too much to add that extra yellow – so be wise when using it. It might upset the mix – turning a piece that does well with more shade into something lighter than it should be.

Carefully know when to use thick yellow in comparison to the joyous regular yellow as we might send the wrong messages. Often giving an anti-climax this hue suggests that everything is all right if not for this and that. Generally fine but something's missing – for me it falls into being a transitional colour that can be used in many ways but lends itself especially to spaces that are not the focal point of an artwork.

When making a statement I would prefer something either faded or more neon, when merely buying space; this hue has a great effect but to use this sparsely usually muddles the mix. I guess you don't want to create that off-beat that this lends. To me it fades the art into a lulled sense of boredom.

Yet I am the expressionistic kind that wants to show off – If you're going for calm and warm this colour will do the trick – brightening those dark areas with a soft knowing of wellbeing.

School Bus Yellow

Unfortunately, I have never taken a trip to school in a yellow bus, but the show made it more believable for when going there every weekday morning to play cards until they came out of my ears like a harlequin.

So many hours spent on figuring out how to win while on the move. On the bus was also my first time to accidentally make a girl fall in love with me – a daunting task that seemed like nothing to me at the time.

I happened to have gotten the opportunity to talk to her while she was alone; and I felt the need to connect with her. Blue-eyed I had a great conversation on that fateful bus which led to complications for her later on. I could never be man enough to be with such a pretty lady.

Nevertheless it's a happy memory I associate with busses, along with the magic school bus TV show that had it miniaturized, flying by, and driving confidently into the futures of so many children.

The colour itself is un-astonishing, unlike its legacy. Yet it makes for a comfortable backdrop and its iconic status has it roll off tongues easily.

I would use it in smaller doses as it does tend to make things mundane quite easily, yet if a more opaque area is your style then I am sure it will do the trick.

I, myself, am more of a statement with eloquence kind of guy, so if you're going to smooth things out by being mellow and awesome at the same time, use this shade.

It does not intimidate, nor does it underwhelm. Tried and true it livens up just slightly – just enough to raise eyebrows a little higher as it does so well at complementing other colours such as green and blue.

A combination with red makes it stun and surprise with danger and a daunting appeal while also making the entire picture be very extreme. I would stay away from using anything more extravagant than a nice orange.

All in all, this hue gives me (and I hope you too), some happy memories of which more shall come when you have children.

Canary

The colour of this bird is astounding – it shows its brilliance and jubilance and is physically manifested in the bird. I cannot help but become happy when my mind glances on such joyfulness.

Full of energy (seemingly coming from nowhere) these birds seem to be happy with the spritely way they are and exude it in their nature-typical fashion of being unworried – nearly stifling fear with attitude.

It's like nothing can bring it down – a force of the wild showing its feathers in an assertive way that catches the eye.

It is to me no wonder that this hue wears such a peaceful bird's name for they really do it proud. So much power in such a small packet, if not for my abysmal feeding ability I would get a canary of my own.

To me things are meant to work on their own and thinking of canaries in the wild; they achieve just that.

As if from a tropical jungle they would sing their chirpy sounds in a manner that instils the knowing of nature being steadfast in harmony.

Oh, how I wish my paintbrush could harness such beautiful magnificence that is the call of nature. I would become enthralled with painting again, yet I leave this to the professionals I admire so and mother nature of course.

All I can do is pay tribute in my way and hope that it sparks interest – share my view and know that somewhere it hits home.

How I wish to be as free as a bird – so much like the canaries in the wild.

To be one of the few/many that roam and are so comfortable in their own skin that it blossoms feathers of such magnitude. They must feel dressed for the occasion every day – as long as the sun is out to let me shine, I would be a frolicking bird.

Lemon Yellow

A hint of it, it only seems but it makes all the difference. Like the taste you get when biting into cake that is meant to taste like butter, it surprises you with fruit.

The ideas that go along with this hue are rejuvenating. Just a spritz and it's all something else.

The work with this colour gives a sense of originality – a hint of flirtatiousness with the tropical. I love using lemon yellow – not only because it is so abundant in the world, but because I have been cultivated to have a liking for it.

It reminds me of pineapples and flowers because there is an inherent deeper connection to what grows and is sour in taste. Tantalizingly it lends itself to a spontaneous character and implies impulsive joy on beaches.

A spruce of life in every use, it awakens the geist to reach for even more. Let's have more fun, let's dance and be merry in a way that is good for us. Let's bathe in what nature has given us and be happy for once– even if only for a few hours.

Making use of this colour I get irritated at too much sour and put the brush down. It mixes well with greens and into greens for obvious reasons but needs to be made use of for its philosophical qualities if you like the life-giving ones.

An air of shallowness that is marked by not thinking deeply into things, I would like to live in a metaphorical river of pine-twist because it has this colour paradoxically.

Just enough sugar to keep me going and enough tang to spark my interest.

Neon Yellow

To start off I choose this colour. It shines without judgement and conjures up dreams most of us have in life. A conversation with all that is and never-ending – symbolically the sun has a special place in our thoughts, being an end and beginning at the same time, the centre of our solar system, the thing the even literally brightens our days and forms so much of our optimistic views.

Seeing the sun as neon is implied to be literal in the sense of being light and also due to the fact that staring at it makes me unable to conceive how something like that (so wonderful and life-giving) could exist to begin with.

Almost all good philosophy can be linked to the sun or yellow because logically it gives life to so much that there is hardly any better comparison.

So, history tells of many who speak of similar things, we have even called our most sacred day the Sunday and the start of our toil (its opposite) the Monday or moon day.

This colour resonates joy with applause and us undeniably a happy one. To such extent that personally I use it to outline some of my patterns in its jovial appearance – I love using neon, and my favourite is neon yellow. No other neon has so much resilience and linearity in its name.

The very use of it puts a smile on my face – my conscience brightens, and it feels as though my heart skips a beat when it glistens.

It's not in-your-face but it enlightens it! To me it's like what they say of blue – subconsciously it raises your mood. For some reason, GIVING reason to be optimistic. It is as if everything inside you starts to conspire to produce positivity instead of other possibility.

Through working with this colour, I have gained so much passively that I can say my basic philosophy is more jubilant simply BECAUSE of the fact that there is NEON yellow. The cherry on top of yellow.

Glowing Yellow

Protruding from my lighter, every time I get to witness a controlled flame with its invigorating effect on me, as joy rushes through me at the sight of an element that is so naturally curated in its movement – swaying in light breezes and instantly reacting to its surrounds at every moment.

I wonder when I see coals stimulated by gas flames, how they slowly burn away, providing an ethereal warmth to the soul. It is such a humbling feeling that fireplaces have become as common as toasters in some households. We need it for the spirit!

Flames in their wild beauty are untameable, as we see on grasslands and woods that cannot withstand being illuminated from the ground up. They make me think of the intrinsic network of energy and how fine it is – nearly not being able to decipher where the nuances of colour mesh into beginnings and endings of slivers of fire.

Flowing lava, the powerful and daunting force from volcanoes, will melt nearly any material in a torrential way that induces fear and paranoia for people living close to such unpredictable features of landscape.

To get close to the crux, glowing yellow is such a delicate but strong force that every filament on a PC screen wants to embody it, yet it is seen mostly in chaotic scenarios that we run from.

Having created instruments that can wield such power, we

seek to be masters over it, failing at transcending its philosophical properties it's like attempting to predict certain futures for changing cultures that evolve with the times at ever increasing rates.

Peaks and slumps will come and go but colours somehow laugh at the face of time – especially when they're as versatile as glowing yellow. It will enlighten any work of art and artist across the world seek to be able to display its qualities as accurately as possible. The poster boy for the hue will always reign supreme, and as we attempt to cage its vibrancy again and again there will be no subduing it.

Our tools cannot evolve beyond a cornerstone of reality. It speaks to needing to go back to basics – so that we always return to a staple of life. An element, like breathing, on which we build our castles in unison with the other elements we seek to replicate in our matrixes.

The dream of recreating reality in our own image – one we are trying to realize yet will have to discard due to sheer impossibility.

Be at ease with the knowledge of changing reality as you go in an unnoticed and also unnoticeable way – without effort and with it in every second and all throughout your life.

We cannot measure our effects on the world, all we know is that is like the energy of the lighter's flame – it's somehow there and all that's left is being in harmony with it. Ever burning.

Burnt Sienna

This hue has a sense being used – having gone through a lot of work or growth there seems to be a significant amount of wear or age along with the marks age inflicts. Like that rusted white car on the scrapyard.

Being a remnant of yellow it reminds me of the nicotine stains on my fingers, while the name lets me think of the South African grasslands burning with black smoke on trips through the plains we have here. There is a deepness in it, which is most probably why it has its own name – sienna, what a gorgeous combination of letters.

With character it displays a precise colour that is also rare. If burnt sienna had a sister, she would be called Savannah – a name just as beautiful as her own and from the same mother, Sierra. Seemingly all from the heritage of terrain the hue lends itself to drawing landscapes – to me especially drawing because of the linear nature.

In my view, specifically well opposed by blue it creates a great contrast for the depiction of a deified lion– the mane signifying speciality, projecting the beast lord over all other beasts. In mythology we see them with wings that are golden along with all the other shades of heavenly yellow in the rest of their body – I see burnt sienna as being similar. For the fact that its name ties to fire – it has survived and bears history, not many hues have that.

The colour is a good middle, apart from its distinct name it is not an extreme of any sort. Malleable, it can be spread onto surfaces that require patterns, yet it is not a centre point of anything. Few will hold high a pinnacle that has this colour, for it underwhelms when put into the spotlight.

It's a team player that makes life easy for reds, bright yellows, and blues – if you would like to shock your audience; pair it with greens, which creates a schism in mind's eyes. When you do add some greens be sure to add some transitional palates so that the difference is not too sudden.

Africa has a very close connection to this colour for the prairie and things that have dried out due to the sun over extended periods of time resonate with burnt. My mind conjures images of smoking grasslands or sunsets with buck grazing – maybe it's because I live here, but deserts do not have the same feel, maybe areas in India, America or Australia could be similar, yet none to me are as synonymous.

As a final note, this colour gives me notions of parchment that is singed at the sides for whatever reason– I have yet to understand why 'wanted' notices bare such marks, but I find that the style is rather fitting in an even-if-I-have-to-write-it, literal sense.

Miscellaneous Browns

To display some humour, I will reveal that I detest browns – they are that which I do not understand. It is life's joke on me to inflict the presence of something that has been through decades and ages of time only to laugh in my face at how naïve and juvenile I am.

Deep brown boasts knowledgeability and pride in a way I cannot describe to anything other than presumptuous and even cocky. Presenting complexities that have not been solved throughout all its life when in my belief there is an antidote to every problem, as long as you put your mind to it.

Spitefully I attribute things that are brown in nature with giving up and being OK with rotting on the outside as long as the inside feels it last. An air of slowly going downhill with the times as death has been accepted as a part of life so that everything can go about its usual cycle.

This philosophy opposes my beliefs due to them being enthusiastically aimed at renewal and the regenerative properties of life.

Brown mocks the use of colour in its unfathomable ways of expressing the myriad of rejuvenating traits exuberance has. By being boring.

To boot, the use of browns is an art on its own – as though there is this culture that revels in the use of this mundane energy to have fun at the toil of boastful hippies with contrary perceptions.

It is the adherence to old in the face of newness, constantly growing into original shapes to somehow thwart the downtrodden beliefs that makes us age.

Fresh leaves grown on brown branches further emphasize the paradox, while at least forming a tree of life.

All I can say is that I seem to need to get a lot OLDER to be harmonic with these shades – maybe I'll even have to start drinking whiskey or brandewein. Innately irritating these thoughts are, because they oppose my entire view – in my core being I have this drive to be released from anything even remotely connected to the opposite of vibrance and spontaneity.

If you want to be content with terrible states of reality you have accepted – you will not and cannot change – then adhere to using brown as a sign of your compliance with slow movements that span decades and ages so that your very mind in itself becomes old and steadfast.

Luckily, we have stones to show how time hones that which is immaturely unwilling to change into pebbles of beauty and roundness.

The invigorating force of water will corrode outmoded beliefs and forgotten life lessons clenched onto will yield to a more complete and energetic way of life that has a greater movement in it than the terribly incessant implication that death is so important, when it is merely a restart button to LIFE.

It nearly goes without saying that my point is that there is only life and death is merely an illusion – please broaden your perspective and see that we can transform our view of brown to be one of comfort in wooden chairs at fireplaces, and the drudge that is the worship of death into the opportunity of reanimation into a better future. Giving rise to the renewable source that recycles and reuses all that which has served its purpose.

Chocolate (cosmos)

This intricate shade is another that speaks to taste in such a deep way. We all know the taste of our favourite snack in the middle of the night and are not unaware of the massive nature that shapes our taste of the cosmos.

To me we are all spiritual travellers in this cosmic plane – we have our own styles, listen to music that fits to us, laugh at only stuff we find funny and do only what makes our hearts truly happy.

Chocolate is probably universal – for if it has not been found on other planets and stars it's only a matter of time.

Like gold, cocoa used to be traded and nowadays we drink it before we go to sleep on romantic evenings of self or with loved ones. It's feel-good.

We invent ways to put chocolate into nearly everything – there is even a colour named after it!

Beyond its nice aroma, I imagine a comfortable couch fashioned in this hue of brown with the TV or fireplace on providing food for thought or vision.

I could look up at the stars and wonder at the cosmos for hours on days I have the patience with myself. Smoothly letting my mind think in a soft and creamy way that benevolently shies away from upsetting thoughts.

How we create our worlds, and how they are entangled in each other like the fabric of a full vestment. Cocoa leaves sprouting from ideas that weave tales through time. How our actions will affect the next generations and how aeons past have shaped ours.

The multiverse is endless and in lives to come we might venture beyond our bodies into spiritual existences far above our current perceptions. If you open your mind to dream there is no telling of what you might achieve but close it and the world is a little darker. Like dark chocolate that is almost bitter...

Dark Green

Being slightly frightened by thorns that bare venom there are plants that have razor sharp edges of their leaves that irritatingly poison you when your skin is pinched by them. I connect such plants with the hue of dark green, for they have evil qualities shrouded in the mystery of shamans from fantastical games that have to do with mystical forces that we do not seek to understand.

Some things are better left alone – the ones that are fascinated with stuff that is not within common understanding are infatuated with being something special that is unpredictable and incalculable.

The qualities of dark green make me think of an evil side to nature, the illnesses it inflicts in defence for survival.

It saddens me that my ally has come to such evolution where it deploys not love, but fearful repercussion to protect itself. So many say that love is the only way, yet here we are confronted with something not of love.

Now who's to say that nature is not being benevolent when administering the knowledge of one needing to stay away from parts of it to find a middle way?

Like attempting to understand a god, I fail at not faltering into the mindset of implying malevolence on behalf of the sinister offspring of nature. Merely being capable of hope I trust that there is always a greater lesson to be learnt when dealing with such a great force.

Delivering intrigue – dark green gives me a sense of it being conniving at its core. Having abundance at a price.

The shadow of deep green, in its nearly evil way, makes me know not to travel too deeply into areas best kept away from my mind's eye – invoking feelings like jealousy and the thought of occurrences such as betrayal.

Few things scare me as much as my own spirit seeking the opposite of own will – internal bipolarism or duality that seeks to torture and stay alive within me. No greater nuisance is there than a behaviour that only subtly gets eroded over time and just refuses to die. It makes me have to chisel at it every day, building this naïve happiness over finally having worn it down a slight bit each time the cycle comes round.

I am incapable of wielding dark green to its fullest extent, yet I find that if you wish to create some hype or infamy then this shade is the way to go. I imagine that leading up to the use of statement-making colours this hue works extremely well.

My philosophy around it is rooted in discreditation, for I am without a different or better defence, so make use of the poison wisely and be sure to make the dose adequate for incapacitation – for it is the only way to render your viewers speechless.

Faded Dark Green

Seemingly haggard, it portraits a weathered exterior – I pull this from the garden furniture I slouch on day in and day out. When the sun hits it, I'm there, thinking of a way I can write in, stones I can use in mosaic and canvases I can ruin with my poor talent.

Dark green gives me the sense of it having been through a lot – like a history book that details all happening in a humble manner, only depicting the things that really matter in an objective fashion.

The patterns it should hold display a subtlety that only it can show. Faded dark green bolsters the scares of being washed by the rain repeatedly to produce an air of strength that it shows boldly.

Not quite unapologetic, not exquisitely humble, not striving to make a statement, not opulent and simply uncaring for lesser topics this hue is not much of anything besides the cornerstone of the colour. In so many words: it is just what it is, and only what it is.

Too often we seek to see what specialities there are in things – what makes them stand out above the crowd? Why do we seek the prominent attributes so readily available? Must everything be handed to us on a platter? This hue is the paradox – it seeks to transcend these notions and just be.

It is, in fact, just being.

If you wish to calm down a work of art, use this hue – it delivers a sense of rest that is unparalleled. Good to be used on bigger surfaces we feel as though we have arrived in a good place. With the absence of expectation and presumption we can ease into our bodies and cultivate being content with ourselves and where our lives are headed.

Brush strokes should leave behind little creases and enamel would make an intricate pattern – mosaic of this sort should be detailed or even empirically flat to show this shade the respect it deserves. What I am getting to, is that dark green needs to be hoisted into a rightful place, not saying that any other should not, but as with everything – it deserves its place.

As all artists dream to make use of all colours in its fitting manner, we can only do our best – they remain tools for our dreams and everyone even dabbling in art will realize there is so much to it. Philosophy integrates and so does proficiency and talent – the list of contributing factors goes on.

So, I reckon what there is to say is that faded dark green has a place in my heart that leaves me be. I stop hounding myself and just relax into a calm know of everything being all right.

Jade

This hue has a mesmerising charm to it. Mystical and powerful, the Aztec mined it for its belief in connection to the afterlife. I am not astounded that it was used in big sculptures before the stairs of temples in the east as it has properties that are said to be very spiritual.

Having a sense of high trade value and great history it gives me the air of high quality and being sought after by merchants of the finest wares.

It has a subtle, but strong character that only slightly falls shy of making a too bold statement.

In the chakra system the heart could be categorized as falling under the colour scheme of jade. An indomitable force that drives our lives with giant need forms cultivation and compassion.

Love mostly being seen with a red shade, the green turns this on its head by introducing care and fragility. Jade rises higher and boasts the heart's greatest values and stands tall doing so.

A great deal of respect I have for those that dress their hearts in such lavish satin, for my fickle heart has yet to learn such patience and benevolence without sacrificing self-respect. Too often do I engage in bargains that put me steps behind when I could be bolder and work up the stamina to outfit my centre with a more resilient demeanour.

There are pictures that I often glance at that involve dress in jade – I look in awe and imagine evenings spent with the people that display it with such splendour and calm. It is not too humble, yet not offensive in any way.

It is as though it has found THE way of being and is comfortable in its own skin, while letting others feel that peace of soul. I wish I had the stillness to be around the ones who I would assign the attributes of being jade spirits in my life – I think I would commune with existence so much better and find wholeness in a far more effortless fashion than the increment of wrongs I take upon myself to battle on a daily basis.

It does hold value to do things your way, but jade has found another one that sees us rise equally with reverence.

Gift Grün

Gift in English means present, reminding of the present being a present that is given to us by life itself, yet gift in German means poison – like venom that is typically fashioned in this shade.

I find the paradox unmistakably intriguing and have long pondered on the subject in my imaginative mind.

I love the concept of the word having different meanings in the two languages and often think of the many poisons that are in the world.

The pufferfish has a poison that paralyses its victims – simulating death in them. This must be the most amazing sensation, to be nearly dead for a while – I wonder what an experience that must be? Does the spirit travel to other worlds, for instance, an origin that we all sprang from, or do we venture to planes of our dreams or is it just like sleep where you simply shut down and wake up once the dose has run its course?

Then there are poisons that cripple, or ones that make you feel ill – ones that drive you insane over a period of time and, then again, others that get you addicted.

On the flipside there are also poisons that cause deliriums or near-death scenarios in which one has a joyous time that stays as an event in one's life one will never forget.

So, there is a sense of poison doing negative things at times, yet there are positive poisons out there – like the analogy of indulging in a desire that has long been yearned for or the completion of an achievement for which dream was the initial venom.

It is a thin line between good and bad that is overstepped when willingly ingesting a concoction that could be bad yet could also be good – it is known that some poisons counteract and nullify certain states of discomfort. Therefore, I see poison as being a medicine in some cases – which brings us back to the paradox that makes it a gift. A gift that synergizes with the present and how we are always faced with the choices within our lives that the present PRESENTS us with – like venom the present is. We are all infused with 'gift' that is sometimes good and at others bad.

So, the choices we make each and every moment change our past, future and present as we change memories, make plans for the future and affect our present quality of life as we move through time and space. It is a journey that, to me, can forever be deciphered and thought about from endless angles and through a myriad of activities reaching from very passive work to work that is deeply involved in determination and drive – almost with utmost impetus, so that the range of ways of being is so great that we have an endless way of being that is uniquely expressed by all the different characters we find in the world.

In my understanding, this is why there is an endless expression of life, and there will always be. Each being follows its self-determined greatest good to arrive at a balance that takes it and the rest of existence that step further in cultivating an energy that is unlike any other. Each individual tailors themselves.

Returning to how this relates to the colour – I find that its biting effect translates into a defensive or offensive affect, much like good and bad, depending on intent. Its hue is sly and mischievous – so full of philosophical interpretation.

Definitely one for eccentric spaces or fierce contrasts, it lends itself to shocking scenes, when injecting the viewer with fear or horror. I imagine many depictions using this colour display something that repulses or makes people feel queasy – so that the nature of poisonous green truly hits its mark.

Not getting the opportunity to use this hue often I like simply meandering around its dualistic properties for moments on end, always returning – that in itself is a poison that I have taken.

Wintergreen Dream

Starting off with mentioning that to me this colour invokes the ideas of many gems, all cut or some natural in so many manners of clean edged all the way to smooth and ruggedly shaped by nature and its tools.

A charismatic calming arises in me when I think of this hue – as if touched by something that has been yearning to show me its beautiful essence. That tendril of life letting me know that here too is something gorgeous and worth knowing about, even exploring when I have gained the elegance and proper respect.

The fact that it is named a 'dream' makes me think its majestic and nearly unfathomable. Yet it exists – to me something rare.

Wintergreen reminds me of surviving it – yet the plants and objects in reality that wear this shade of green all seem to trump winter in a way that shows resilience and stature.

All together it gets me thinking of unique and strong aspects that withstand the tests of time and make it through trouble with strength of character.

Dreams also give me the air of coming true in forms undiscovered and surprising – as if being marbled and unchangeable while having a knowing of being there for the taking but needing the work to get to. Keep on going and working at those dreams and you shall live them – instead of them being something you achieve once and exploding away as if they were flashbangs.

It also gives me the sense of being wise – so many teachers say that dreams are built out of many tiny steps that culminate into something bigger. I must say that it is a way of life. Baby steps become small steps and so time goes on and later getting up and running with enthusiasm is a daily act.

So, we grow, flourish and whither in such a variation of ways – so many unseen and unnoticed because no one told us that we are soaring through life – it's just kind of normal...

Magic Mint

Having a sense of being the luminescent shine that comes off the ponds beneath small waterfalls in a secluded part of woodlands where fairies bathe, this colour already has magic within it.

Its name invokes wonder and awe as it promises eye-opening experience into taste sensations of the powerful herb. As I am sure mint is used in alchemy for better taste and other benefits this shade of green mixed with white has a somewhat delicate feel to it – as if softly giving hints to the tongue as tiny stars that emanate from its energy touch it when eating.

I would pair this with soft other colours that contrast or complement it, such as a light pink or a hazy blue.

It is not as versatile as other colours yet can also be used to accentuate in small doses.

I find it to lend itself to milky areas that motion toward infinity and the endless spirals and horizons that life presents.

Much like a soft blue it would strongly contrast etchings and highly detailed drawings and when worn in clothing would deliver a soothing notion of harmlessness and meekness.

Like a forest fawn shortly after birth – still fragile but willing to walk until finally jumping around in joy between green leaves on meadows.

There are few hues that lend such a soft touch – almost like dandelions in the sun or on grassy knolls it gives rise to ease of life and a worriless existence some can only dream of.

I would not bother pairing this colour with black for fear of a bee pattern effect because of their different natures yet in extreme circumstance it would be possible to get such a shrill effect. It might seem daunting, and as a hint I would advise to feel the flow of a colour before getting into such climaxes between opposing shades that often get me perplexed in the middle of practicing my art.

Celebrating calm is what this hue is all about – enjoying its feel and likening it to all the wonderful experiences you have had in your life…

Turquoise

Being my favourite colour sometimes I smirk, I am in a sea of infatuation with the myriad of hues there are in the world. I never know which one I love the most at any given time.

Passively I wish I could write about them all at once, I reckon that is why my art always turns out to be too colourful. Yet turquoise somehow grasps the sense of creativity better than others. It blends and twists into washes and shimmers as the stones on my mosaic pieces glisten in the sun and my poor acts of trying to mix into it fail to produce a new version every time.

It has an air of vibrance along with a subtlety that only it can express.

I find endless joy at contrasting turquoise with the other colours because there is so much individual life that it provides. The combination of happy and content with alive and spontaneous.

When I touch upon it, I want to find precise pieces I can use it on and only the ones that lend themselves to its use get to be decorated in it.

Being one that needs to be shown for all its grandeur it feels good to use it on centrepieces and bigger surfaces. It grips the mind with its surprising speciality and never disappoints me.

It is a joy to see it in nature (even though that might be a rare sight), it reminds me of seeing butterflies.

To go deeper – I kind of have a good feeling in my tummy right now.

Often fading green into blue, you might be lucky enough to glance upon turquoise, yet it takes the cake! So, stay away if you want to let the others shine... Jewels should all be likened to this hue for that is how highly I regard it. Deep splendour and sincere conveyance of what is unique this delivers in style and with confidence.

Not unapologetic and still humble.